RELUCTANT SOULS

KELLY MICHAEL VELAYAS

Reluctant Souls
Copyright © Kelly Michael Velayas

First edition 2020

Edited by Bonnie Hearn Hill
Cover design by Rose Miller

This is a work of fiction, nothing that this story relates to is true, in any form or manner. Any resemblance of actual people, places or happenings is purely coincidental.

Dedicated to Paula

O livro é minha despedida, ta.

Pieces of the Puzzle

—*Childhood Memory*

Santa Fe, New Mexico

Adult voices...Blah...blah...blah...

A cowboy hat on the shelf – toy gun too!

Reach out – mine!

Giant strangers everywhere – pounding the floor with heavy feet!

Adult voices – angry and mean.

I touched it...Am I doing something wrong?

Oh well!

But the shiny gun – metallic – ready to shoot! Bang! Bang! And the hat – where's a mirror? Where?

Waylon sings on the radio, about good old boys.

Oh no! Grandma – finger pointing – angry – angry – always angry.

She grabs me – saying something...

Okay, okay! Just let go.

She's gone again!

Gun – gun! Hat! Look at me, a cowboy!

Serious now – just like John Wayne and Lee Marvin!

Wait. Someone!

Turn around slowly

Hello!

Who is she?

A girl!

She's staring – lashes long and curious.

Think – think...

What?

Is she looking at me?

Why can't I stop looking at her?

Who is she?

Look down, then back up.

She's still smiling!

Her eyes...Is she – is she?

What is pretty – her?

Is she pretty or beautiful?

Dark hair – large – studying – staring eyes.

She understands things.

Yes, she's beautiful.

She's so serious – glancing – changing thoughts – angry?

She won't turn away.

She walks closer.

Oh my!

Angry voices again! Who? Her mom – not Grandma! Serious – waving finger. Blah...blah...blah...

Her mom pulled her around the corner!

Leave her alone – mean mom!

Back to my toys... A toy – toy? Never mind!

Where is she – the girl?

Follow her – peak around.

There she is – staring back. She sees me!

Run? No. Look again! There she is – still staring!

The adults left.

Her eyes…her eyes…

My eyes…

She smiles again.

I stare right back – don't turn away. She's nervous like me. Look – her breathing.

What does love mean?

Dress – long hair – eyes?

I'm sweating!

Look at her! Her feet. Sandals. Soft. Light…

What's her name?

Her mom's back, pulling her away again – those mean adults!

Blah…blah…blah…they say over and over again.

She's searching for me!

Look! Here I am!

She finds me – her soft smile.

Follow her. Out the store – down the sidewalk.

Adult voices – who? Mine! Grandma – angry!

"Don't you dare go outside!"

Grandma can be mean…

I have to go back in.

She's gone. Who was she?

Where did she go?

Bye, bye…

—*A Farewell*

"GRANDAD WOULD WANT THE MEN. Go ahead."

Young Dallas, Uncle Cam, a cousin, and Don Junior, another uncle who was younger than Dallas all stepped over a rail, and carefully climbed down the boulders.

Cam, the eldest, carried a small box.

A golden eagle circled above. Clouds hung low in the distance far away from them. The canyon's jagged stones scraped upward, and bushes dotted its face. The Snake River turned over and over, cascading down the green valley as prairie grass waved in the breeze.

All the men, their hands steady, were aware this was the moment. Now, they'll only be left with their memories, their link to the past; those days on Pismo Beach with Great Grandma, rafting down the Snake, that summer in Jackson Hole, Sunday mornings at the Baptist church with hands raised to God. They remembered all the looks, their grandpa, their father, their friend, his fingers prying their mouths open, staring in, making sure their teeth were clean and cared for. The man who lived under a bridge during the depression, married his high school sweetheart, had five children, and then abandoned their mother because, he said, she used sex to manipulate him. He gave up his job, threw away millions in real estate to become a roofer and rodeo cowboy in Wyoming. He told stories of Harrison Ford and Tom Selleck knocking men out at the Cowboy Bar. Then, in his fifties, he married a woman half his age and had two more children. He became a legend, an outfitter, and a professional drunk.

Cam opened the lid.

They all reached out, holding the box.

"Goodbye, Father."

"Bye, Grandad."

"Bye, Grandpa."

Cam looked to everyone. "Ready?" he asked.

"Bye, Dad," barely came out of Don Junior's mouth. Tears streamed down his cheeks.

The men all nodded, except Don Junior.

Cam slowly turned the box. Ashes trickled out.

Then, he turned it upside down, and ashes poured.

Don Junior knelt, holding his stomach in pain.

The others watched both the ashes and him.

"It's okay," Cam told him.

The boy could neither speak, nor look. His eyes were closed as tightly as possible. Dallas felt for him. He watched as some ashes took flight. Most of them just fell to the ground. A cloud of dust built around their hands.

Junior coughed. He just couldn't stop crying.

A bolt of lightning shot in a tiny streak above the canyon wall far in the distance, too far for the thunder to be heard.

The eagle continued to circle.

Cam and Dallas patted Don Junior's back.

"It's okay. It's okay," they said, even though they knew he would not recover. The mentally and physically handicapped boy had lost his father, his best friend, his everything.

Dallas held Don Junior's hand, helping him up the rocks and back over the rail. Then, Dallas turned and faced the canyon. Just then, he remembered his grandad spanking him after he caught Dallas inside a girl's sleeping bag.

Dallas was twelve, and the girl was thirteen. But Grandad took responsibility for her. The girl's parents, friends of Dallas's aunt, let her take the trip out to the coast, which was common back then.

How did Grandad explain that to her parents? Dallas wondered.

He looked to the ground and then up to the sky – the eagle – the endless blue. And then he waved.

"Bye, Grandad Walling."

—*Makin' Things Right*

FIVE THIRTY IN THE MORNING – still dark – Dallas paced outside his truck. His cowboy boots beat the wet asphalt.

Thirty minutes. Nothing.

One hour. Nothing.

At 6:45, a car drove through the parking lot. The man behind the wheel gave him a hesitant wave.

Dallas walked back to his truck and took a seat, leaving the door open.

He pulled his worn-out baseball cap down over his eyes and ran his fingers through his goatee.

Seven spaces down, a car parked.

The cowboy. Dallas looked to see if he recognized the driver. Was it a man, or a woman?

Whoever it was, they were on their cellphone.

The door opened.

A man.

He got out, glanced in the cowboy's direction, and didn't say a word. Then he walked to the front door, pulled out a set of keys, unlocked it, and went inside.

Lights turned on throughout the building. Dallas saw the man's silhouette against the panes of glass.

More time went by.

The sun was coming up, and the sky turned a soft blue. Another car arrived and then an SUV, both drivers talking on their phones. They hung-up as they exited their vehicles and went straight into the building. Men. No women.

The cowboy just sat there, watching.

A black car came into the parking lot and stopped directly across from Dallas.

That looks like a woman...

She sat in the car, talking on the phone, continuously glancing over her shoulder at the cowboy.

He didn't take his eyes off her.

This might be it.

She finally got out from her car.

No. Not her.

The woman stood for a brief moment, staring at the cowboy as he sat in his truck. She grinned and then walked into the office building, giggling.

By seven thirty, she should be here.

Seven-thirty came.

Then seven forty.

Seven-forty-five.

Seven-fifty.

Seven-fifty-five.

At exactly eight, a black Lexus rolled into the parking lot and parked two spaces down from the cowboy.

He stared at the car. Nobody got out.

His fingers tapped his thigh.

Eight-O-one.

Eight-O-two.

Eight-O-three.

Eight-O-four.

This might be her. I know she's the boss.

The cowboy thought back. She was tough, straightforward. Over the sixteen years – he'd sifted through every detail, every smile, every gesture, phrase, every mean thought. She was bold, easy to read.

Yeah, she would park near me.

She had aged, gotten stronger, and like a good manager, she would take on responsibility. It had to be her.

But don't do anything until she leaves her car.

At 8:05, a woman stepped-out of the Lexus, no makeup, hair loose. She glared at the cowboy, gaze darting downward, and then back up again.

My God! There she is! It's her!

Dallas stood and took a couple of steps in her direction.

"What are you doing?" she demanded, her voice breaking.

Her words stopped him in his tracks.

Remember the deal…

"Do you want me to leave?" he asked.

"I want you to leave me alone!" she shot back.

Dallas looked down, into his truck. He reached for the door.

He had promised he'd go, without question, not say word.

A deal's a deal.

"Okay," he said.

Dallas got back into his truck, backed-up, glanced at her one last time, and drove away.

His hands trembled over the steering wheel.

This is life. Just keep going through it like you always have. Just keep going.

Turn signal.

Look.

Don't hit that car.

Red light.

Stop.

Green light.

Go.

Dallas kept driving, trying not to think about what had just happened.

As he was getting onto the tollway, his phone rang.

Dallas didn't recognize the number but knew from the area code, it was local to Clearwater.

Is it her?

I've got to answer.

"Hello."

"This is the Sheriff's department. Is this the individual who just left International Plaza?"

"Yes, sir," Dallas said.

"Where are you at this very moment?"

"I'm not sure. I'm driving, about to get onto a tollway. Are you back at the building?"

"Yes. Go ahead and pull over and tell me where you are – exactly – the intersection, the cross streets."

"You want me to go back to the building, sir?" Dallas asked.

"No. Just pull over."

"You can trust me. I'll go back if that's what you want."

"How far away are you?"

"I'm about ten – fifteen minutes," Dallas said.

"Fifteen minutes?"

"Yes, sir."

"Okay. Do not come to the front of the building. Park to the side."

Ten minutes later, the cowboy was approaching the building.

A police car screeched around the parking lot.

The moment the cowboy saw the squad car, he stopped his truck.

Once you've been arrested, you know the drill. He did.

Dallas took the keys from the ignition, walked behind the truck, placed the keys and his wallet on the ground behind him. Then, he put his hands on the tailgate and stared at the ground, so the officer knew he wasn't a threat.

The cop drove up and pulled around him. The officer got out and approach Dallas from behind, he said, "Keep your hands there."

"I know. I'm ready to go to jail, sir."

He kept taking deep breaths, narrowing his eyes, flaring his nose, blinking.

The scene kept playing out in his head, the words.

I should've said more, but a deal's a deal. Now, I'm going to jail, and I never told her what I wanted to say.

And now I go to jail.

The officer found nothing in his pockets. Then, he picked up his wallet and pulled out his license.

"From Texas?"

"Yes Sir."

"Is this your current address?"

"Yes, sir."

"The sheriff will be here in a moment."

"Yes, sir."

A minute later, the sheriff pulled-up and parked behind them.

The sheriff got out of his car. He was enormous and hard-muscled with bicep tattoos, probably a former football player.

The deputy nodded.

"Okay. Sir, step away from the truck. Come here."

Dallas turned and slowly approached the sheriff.

"What are you doing?" he asked Dallas. "What just happened?"

"I had to see her, sir," said Dallas.

"What?"

"I had to look in her eyes."

"You had to look in her eyes?" The sheriff didn't turn from Dallas, and he knew the big man was watching his every move.

"I hadn't seen her in sixteen years. I promised I'd see her in Brazil, and I stood her up. I wanted her to know that it was a mistake. I had to prove it…I just had to see her eyes, in person."

The sheriff frowned. "Hope it was worth it."

"Even if I go to jail," he said.

"Maybe I understand." The sheriff nodded, and for a moment, he looked as if he might smile. "It's a shame the law don't."

"Yes, sir."

"A lot is on this, cowboy."

"I understand."

"How did you get her phone number and the address of her workplace?"

"The wrong way."

The sheriff nodded.

"Did she tell you not to come?"

"Yes, sir." No point lying.

"Did she tell you that you were harassing her?"

"Yes, she did."

The sheriff pulled out his handcuffs.

Dallas took a deep breath.

"Okay. You're under arrest. Turn around. Put your hands behind your back."

"Even if I die in jail, sir." Dallas took another breath. "It was worth it."

"Okay," The sheriff read him his rights. "You have the right to remain silent. Anything you say, can and will be used against you in a court of law. You have the right to talk to a lawyer and have them present with you while you're being questioned. If you cannot afford a lawyer, one will be appointed to represent you before any questioning, if you wish. You can decide at any time to exercise these rights and not answer any questions or make any statements."

Then, the sheriff placed Dallas in the back of the deputy's squad car. Dallas closed his eyes and tried to control his breath.

Yup!

Just like this…

—4

ALARM – SNOOZE – OFF. Get up – makeup – dress – kitchen – coffee – toast – bite – run – no – jog to the car – stop – spilling coffee – walk fast – get in – drive – get out – go into the building – smile – hello – hello – hello – shake a hand – don't forget to smile at him – he's the boss – okay – on time – sit – go through paperwork – talk with employees – men and women in suits – frustration – stupid – incompetent – no one pays attention – all their hunger – all their lies – little – white – obvious.

"Gabi, the printer isn't working! We can't do anything!"

"I'll call someone."

Gabi picked up the phone, "Hello! Is this Raul in the service department? Can someone come up and fix our printer?"

Must get production. What to do? Calm – calm – calm – order and calm…

Gabi sat down in the cafeteria to eat her lunch, healthy food, counting each calorie. Can't eat too much. Just a quarter of an inch will show…

Finally, the day was over.

Home.

She stared out the apartment window, the endless afternoon, light reflecting, filtered in through transparent curtains, bright but somehow also dim.

A breeze bent tree branches. Feet stepped without sound under the patio fence.

Rows of short three-story boxes stretched forever: apartment, apartment, apartment...

Millions, everyone in the same living room, turned away from the same black box. *Jeopardy, Wheel of Fortune*, baseball, *Leave it to Beaver*, rerun, rerun. Everyone looking out the same window, dreaming the same dream.

She picked up the phone and dialed a number. The phone rang and rang.

She thought the endless thoughts that fill a mind when left alone. *Stay positive. Plan the future, forget the past and its failures. Grow mentally, get stronger.*

Where she was, she at least had calm and order, but somewhere else, she couldn't predict.

She picked up the phone and dialed the number. Still no answer.

~   ~   ~

At the other end of the line, a man stared at his phone.

"Who is it?" asked a girl.

"My wife," he said.

—5

JOGGING – SHE STARED at an old man and woman. They were kissing.

To her right, a woman holding a phone, was crying. She walked across a street, heard a car horn honking and jumped out of the way just in time.

Still trembling, she ran by an outside bar and stopped to catch her breath. She made her way through the maze of chairs, found a secluded table, looked at a beer on a table, but ordered water.

From the bar, a tall man glanced her way and smiled. Another said something. She turned away.

A short, wrinkled woman with white animal hair—a dog or cat—on her navy-blue coat was handing out cards.

"Hello, young lady," she said to Gabi.

Before Gabi could smile back, the woman handed her a card. At the same time, the server placed Gabi's bottle of water on her table.

"Hello," Gabi said.

"What's your name, sweetheart?"

"Gabriela."

"Such a pretty name for such a lovely lady."

"Thank you."

"Gabriela, you dial this number, give a nickname, and you talk with people, preferably men."

"Oh, I see," Gabi gave her what the elderly women wanted, a knowing smile and laugh.

"They call from all over the country, you know?"

"Oh, is that right?" Gabi couldn't help but grin.

"Yes," said the woman. "Exotic men!"

"Oh, they're exotic?"

Their gazes met. They couldn't help but connect, and just for a moment, Gabi saw something familiar. A mother, a grandmother, maybe a fear, a scary future.

"You look like you need to call, sweetheart," the woman said.

"Oh, I do, do I?"

"I know these things, sense them. It's on your face." She winked.

"Yeah, sure it is." Gabi laughed again and shook her head.

The older woman patted her on the shoulder and walked away.

Gabi tapped the plastic table with her fingernails, staring at the woman as she left, carefully navigating, looking into eyes, searching for kindness.

Gabi looked at her watch. It was late. She got up, paid for the water, and went to the trash to throw the card away.

A man stepped out, blocking her. She tried to step around him. The man smiled.

Gabi looked up and rolled her eyes.

What an asshole!

She put the card away and left.

—6

HEAT UP MICROWAVE DINNER, sit down, take a bite, nervous for some reason. Dial the number.

It rang five times.

Trevor answered.

"Finally!" said Gabi. "I've been trying to talk to you for days. How are you?"

"Fine."

"Good. How are the classes?"

"Gabi, I'm really busy."

"Oh, okay."

"I gotta go, okay?"

"Yeah, yeah. No, that's fine. I understand. Love you!"

Dial tone.

Gabi went through her phone's contacts. She wanted to talk to someone who was interested in her. Right in front of her was Gen's number. "Sis!" she thought. Perfect.

The phone rang three times before Gen picked up.

"Hello, Sissy," said Gen.

She sounded distracted.

"Hello, Gen." said Gabi. "My God, you won't believe it!"

"Believe what?" Gen asked her. "Doesn't sound good."

"How'd you know?" Gabi said.

"We're sisters. I had to get out of the house too."

"What's it about today?" Gabi asked

"I don't know, Sis. I can't talk now. I'm on a date, watching a movie."

They said their goodbyes, and Gabi hung up and tried another number, but only getting her friend's answering machine.

She put her food down for her dog to eat. He wouldn't touch it. She stared out the window, and when she turned, she knocked over her purse. Its contents spilled over the floor.

Sigh.

She picked up lipstick, a comb, mirror, and assorted receipts, putting everything back inside. Then, she saw it.

Look! The card...

Oh my God! I didn't throw it away.

Gabi stared. Then, she laughed.

She grabbed the phone and dialed the number, still laughing!

What am I doing?

The phone rang twice.

"Welcome to the connection hotline," said a female computer voice.

Gabi couldn't stop laughing, "Oh, lovely!"

"Hello!" said a woman. A real, live one this time.

"Hi," Gabi told her. She wanted to say she'd never done anything like this before, wanted to say she wasn't crazy, but she knew probably everyone who called the line said something like that.

"Men, or women?" the woman asked.

"What?" Gabi pulled the phone from her ear.

The operator repeated, "Do you want to speak with men or women?"

"Um, I don't know. Just anyone. Just a little. That's all."

"Men. Nickname, please?"

"My name?"

"No, a nickname…"

"Gabi."

"Okay. Good etiquette, no cursing," the woman said. "Don't give out your personal information. You don't know who you're talking to – anyone, from all over the country."

"I understand." Oh, my God, she was really doing this, she thought.

"Press 1 to switch to another man, and when you're done, just hang up. You'll be charged per minute."

"Okay," Gabi said.

"Goodbye. Good luck!"

"Thank you. I think…"

A computer voice said, "Joey44."

"Hello…Hello…Hello…" said an anxious-sounding man.

Gabi laughed and pressed 1.

Computer voice, "James Learner."

"Hello?"

"Hi," said Gabi.

"So, where ya from?"

Gabi pressed 1.

The computer voice, "Daryl T."

"Hello babe…"

1.

Computer voice, "Macho Man."

"Hello?"

"Hi," said Gabi.

"Want to go out?"

Oh God!

"Loser!"

1.

"This is the last one…"

The computer voice said, "Garfield32."

There was silence.

"Hello?" said Gabi.

"Yes," said a man.

"You think you're Garfield the cat?" Gabi asked.

There was no response.

"This is a waste of time…" She laughed.

"Meow," said the man.

"So, who am I talking with?" she asked.

"My name is Garfield."

"What's your real name?"

"Does it matter?" the man said. "Are you pretty?"

"Does it matter?" Gabi shot back.

"I guess that's my point," he said. "It doesn't."

"You're probably 300 pounds without front teeth, and everyone calls you Bubba!"

"Das right ma'am," he replied.

"Really?" Gabi asked.

"Oh please," he said. "I'm only 299 pounds, and I got one front tooth!"

"You're bad," she said. "You like to lie?"

"No. Actually I don't lie."

"I wonder what you're really like," she said. "What type of person calls an 800 number to pick up girls?"

"A pretty desperate one," he replied. "Of course, I could ask you the same question."

"Except I'm not trying to pick up someone."

"I'm not either."

They continued their exchange, and Gabi continued to ask his real name. No way was it Garfield. The more he evaded the question, the more frustrated she became.

Finally, he said. "I don't go by my real name anyway. You'd hate it!"

"Well, I'll be the judge of that." She glanced out the window and realized it was almost dusk. They'd been talking for longer than she realized.

Feet stepped beneath the fence again. The trees were motionless. She looked at the clock and saw it was almost seven o'clock.

"What's your name, dude?" she asked again.

"Dude?"

"Yeah," she said.

"You'll never know, but I know yours, Gabriela!"

Her face flushed when she realized she hadn't bothered making up a nickname."

"I wouldn't use my real name, Garfield," she said.

"But you did."

"I have to go. Nice talking with you, whoever you are!"

"Okay, Gabriela!"

Gabi couldn't help but smile.

She hung up, and then stared out the window again. The rows of apartments blocked the sunset.

—7

GABI AWOKE TO a phone call.

She spoke into the receiver. "Hello? Honey?"

"Gabi, wake up! You're late! Where are you? Meeting starts in ten minutes!"

"Jennifer? Oh my God! What time is it?"

She looked at the clock. "Almost nine! I couldn't sleep. Okay Jenny. Bye. Gotta go!"

She practically fell out of bed. A little makeup and some clothes, and she was out of there, running to her Chevy Cavalier.

She lived ten minutes from her job. She sped down East Green Street, right here, left, right, right again, park!

She ran up the stairs, telling herself, *calm, calm, must be presentable,* and walked into the meeting.

"Sorry I'm late," she said and took a seat.

The meeting resulted in nothing – as usual.

The day ticked away, with each digit of the clock.

Who cares about work!

For the first time in my life, I just don't care!

At five, she rushed home.

Gabi waited for 6:45. Then, she dialed the number.

"Franklin24"

1.

"Jaws"

1.

"Paulanka9"

1.

"Doggy Style"

1.

"Stalin"

Oh God!

1.1.1.

"Brian"

1.

"Diver Jones."

1.

"Eric."

1.

"Richard call me dick."

1.

"Slick Mick."

1.

"Bad Sleep Well."

1.

"Hot Dogger."

1.

"Go4."

1.

"I give up!" She hung up.

Think. Think.

She walked away from the phone. Then, she came back and called again.

The computer voice said, "Garfield32."

Her heart stopped.

"Hello?"

"Yes."

"Garfield...the Garfield?"

"One and only!"

There was a long silence.

"Gabriela? The, Gabriela? Fancy meeting you here!"

"So...so...where are you? I bet you're a thousand miles away."

"I'm working in Illinois. Don't know what the heck I'm doing here. You sound exotic. You on a tropical beach?"

Another long silence.

"I can't believe you're in Illinois," she said.

"You too? What are you doing here?"

"What part of Illinois are you in?" Gabi ran her hand through her hair as if he could see her, but that was crazy. He was still just an unfamiliar voice on the phone. Still, not as unfamiliar as before.

"I'm down south, near Saint Louis."

"I'm in Chicago," said Gabi.

"But, I'm not from here," he said. "Just working."

"I'm not from here either," she told him. "I'm from Brazil. What about you?"

"All over. I've lived and worked in – I don't know – ten or eleven states," he said. "What part of Brazil are you from?"

"São Paulo."

"What part?"

"Do you know São Paulo?" she asked.

"Oh yeah," he said.

"I'm from Tatuapé."

"That was the first metro station I went to when I arrived. I lived near there."

Here, Gabi had resorted to an 800 number, and she had met someone who seemed to have more in common with her than the people she saw every day.

"I can't believe it," she said.

"Believe it."

"Now, will you tell me your real name?"

"Everyone calls me Dallas or Dal." He paused, and when she didn't respond, he asked, "What's yours?"

"Everyone calls me Gabi." Then, before she could think better of it, she asked, "Dallas, are you for real?"

"I don't know. Maybe Einstein or Shakespeare could answer that. I think I am. How about you?"

"I'm real."

"I want you to know this, right now," he blurted. "Okay?"

"Okay."

"Gabi, I'm married."

He was being honest. She had to do the same.

"So am I," she said.

"Okay."

"You're married to a Brazilian?" she asked.

"Yes," he said.

"How old are you?"

"Twenty-six. And you?"

"Twenty-eight," she said.

"Wow."

"So, Dallas, do you speak Portuguese?"

"A little," he said.

"You even speak my language!"

"Yes."

"Is this for real?"

"I don't know."

"What are we doing?" she asked. "Calling strangers in the night."

"I don't know."

"Yeah. It's crazy, I meet someone like you – here. We're even in the same state," Gabi said. "Where else have you been?"

"I worked in Venezuela – Caracas – all over the country really, before it became communist," he said. "Well, it was turning communist when I was there."

"I've been there too."

"I lived on Margarita Island."

"I went to Caracas on a business trip," Gabi said. "Then I went to see the island. Isn't this crazy? We've been to the same places."

"Really crazy. Did you go to the island by yourself?"

"Yes, I did," she told him. No point in lying.

"Do you do everything by yourself?" he asked.

"Pretty much."

"Yeah. Me too."

She paused for a moment and then asked, "Dallas?"

"Yes?"

"Are you a womanizer?"

"Are you a slut, Gabi?"

"No." She gasped. "I can't believe you said that!"

"Why not?" He chuckled. "Let's get serious, okay?"

"Okay."

"Do you want a big-fat one?" Dallas laughed.

Gabi covered the phone and smiled to herself.

"That's not funny! That's sad!"

"No, it's funny." Dallas kept laughing. "You love it."

Gabi suppressed a giggle, but she did feel herself smile.

"I'm sorry," Dallas said. "If I were a womanizer, would it matter?"

"Yes, it would," she said.

"Oh. Well, I'm not."

"I doubt that, Dallas."

"Does it change things?"

This was getting them nowhere. She sighed and said, "I have to go."

"Are we going to talk again?" Dallas asked.

"I don't think so," she told him. "This is getting dangerous."

"Ah, but you're from Brazil! São Paulo! Danger is your middle name!" he said.

"Oh, you think so?"

"What's your number?" he asked.

"Why?"

"To talk," he said. "Why else?"

—8

GABI JOGGED, out of breath. She stopped and stared down a street, – past cars and buildings, and then, back the other way.

The song on her Walkman was Nickelback's, *This, is How You Remind Me.*

Gabi's mind was still into the lyrics, singing an eloquent dream, but she had to wake up or she'd go deeper into her trance and become completely lost.

"How can this be? Did I take a wrong turn?"

She walked to a hotel and asked the concierge if she could go inside.

"Yes. Go ahead," he said.

"Thanks!"

Gabi walked in, and the man followed her to the maps on the wall.

She looked at the city map. The concierge walked away. She went to the state map, and then the larger US map. Her finger ran down I-55, past Springfield to Saint Louis. She took a deep breath and then traced the route down I-44 to Oklahoma City. And then, down I-35 to Dallas, Texas.

~   ~   ~

Dallas was forty feet up in the air, cutting into a pine tree, his chainsaw screaming, breaking wood. A branch tumbled to the ground and landed near a man. Ryan.

Dallas looked down. Ryan stared up, pointing to his eyes and then to Dallas.

Dallas shrugged and continued cutting, concentrating on his chainsaw.

Jimmy yelled and waved his hands, "Dal. Dal."

Dallas stopped cutting when he saw his friend.

"Come on," Jimmy shouted. "Lunch."

Dallas climbed down, spikes ripping into the trunk, his hands barely touching the bark, his strap rolling down the tree as he went, step by step.

"You didn't give the sign, Dallas."

"I know. Don't ask."

They walked toward the mess tent, two men, Ryan and another guy, following behind them.

"They got Philly cheese steaks today," said Jimmy, looking over his shoulder.

The men behind them mumbled.

Dallas looked at Jimmy, who just shook his head.

Ryan threw a soda cap at Dallas, hitting his neck.

"Nervous, Dal?" Ryan asked.

Dallas stepped aside. Jimmy stopped beside him.

"Go ahead, Ryan," said Dallas.

Ryan walked between them. Then, he stared directly into Dallas's eyes. Dallas didn't turn away.

"You're used to steppin' aside?" Ryan asked. "Wife trained ya good."

"Hey Ryan, a simple question for you," Dallas replied, "nothing too complex, okay? Just something straight forward. A yes or no will suffice."

"Ask away." Ryan stopped and faced him.

"Do you suck dick?" Dallas pulled down his zipper and undid his belt buckle. "Just asking, sir. You got a pretty mouth. No hard feelings, right? You do a good job, I let you do it again."

Ryan ran at Dallas, but Jimmy got between them. Ryan swung, but his friend pulled his arm back.

Dallas laughed and buckled his pants back up.

"Hey, Ryan."

"Shut up, Dallas." said Jimmy.

Ryan jumped at Dallas, but again, his friend yanked his arm.

Dallas stepped back.

The two stared at each other.

"Motherfucker, you land a log near me again, I'll end you," Ryan said.

"It was an accident, Ryan," Jimmy insisted. "No one got hurt."

"Hey, Jimmy," Ryan said. "Pull your friend's head out of your ass, or you'll go with him."

"Just calm down," said Jimmy. "Let it go."

"Come on, Ryan," said his friend.

"Dallas." Ryan shouted. "Stay clear of me."

"Oh, that's the way it is?" said Dallas.

Ryan and his friend walked on, but Dallas could tell Ryan still wasn't finished. "Think about it, Jimmy." Ryan yelled, as his friend pulled him away.

Jimmy put his arm around Dallas' shoulder and turned him in the opposite direction. "Man. You need to stop."

"Yeah. Maybe."

"There ain't no maybe. You can't fight everyone, Dallas."

Jimmy stared back at Ryan until they were out of sight. Dallas was shaking.

Jimmy pulled him around and looked into his eyes.

"What the fuck happened, Dal? He's right. You almost killed him. Everyone saw it. It's not good."

Dallas looked down, "I don't know what's wrong with me."

"Man, go home. Get something. Fuck. You know that ain't the last of that."

"Yeah, I know."

"Okay. Well, you know what they say." Jimmy grinned.

Both of them recited at the same time, "All work and no play makes Jack a dull boy."

—9

"THIS IS SO CRAZY. I don't even know you, Gabi said. "I haven't even seen you."

"Yeah."

"We talk every night," she said.

"I know," Dallas said quietly.

"What do you want?"

"I don't know."

"What's wrong, Dallas? You're not yourself."

"Nothing."

"Something's wrong. Did something happen at work?"

"No."

"Is it because you're going home?"

"Maybe. I don't know. Maybe work, maybe everything."

There was a long silence.

"Maybe…" said Dallas.

"What can I say?"

"I don't know."

"I want to tell you something," she said.

"Wait…Gabi?"

"Yes?"

"Open your shirt," he said.

"What?"

"Just a little."

There was a very long silence – deep breathing.

"Don't do this," said Gabi.

"Please, for me."

"I've never done this over the phone," she said.

"Do it."

"I don't like this stuff. I'm not like that Dallas."

"Do it for me."

"No."

"Please…"

Cloth ruffled.

"Okay," she told him. "It's open."

"It is?"

"Yes. What do you want?"

A long silence.

"Do it," he said.

"We're going very deep," she whispered.

"I know."

"Oh, my gosh, my heart is racing."

"Yes."

"What should I do?" she asked.

"You know what to do. Think of me."

"I don't even know what you look like, Dallas."

"I told you," he said.

"But I haven't seen you."

"Yeah. I know."

"Okay, but I want you to do it too."

"I will."

"Oh, my God," she said.

"Can I hear you?" he asked. "Do it."

"Shut up. I am." Her voice broke.

"I want to hear you."

"Your wife doesn't do this, does she?"

"No," he said.

"That's what I thought."

There was silence, just heavy breathing.

"I love you Dallas. I can't believe I just said that. I haven't even seen you."

There was another long silence, but it was good. They didn't have to say anything; they were connected. They knew what was happening. The gravity of their words and actions were entering their souls.

"I have so much to say," she told him.

"Yes. Me too."

"I can't believe you're going home."

"I've got to," he said. "I have a son."

"Yeah. I know."

"You understand?" he asked.

"Yes. I just can't believe it."

"Yeah. Me too."

"If you have to go, then go," she said.

"Okay?"

"Does it matter what I say?" She began to cry.

"What do you want?" he asked.

"Later," she told him. Bye."

"Don't do this," he said. "Don't hang up like this."

"Bye, Dallas," Gabi slammed the phone down.

~ ~ ~

"Damn. Damn." Gabi sobbed. She got up, stared out that same window at the same trees, the same fence, and the same feet walking by.

—10

EARLY MONDAY MORNING, Dallas stepped out into the sunlight with his coffee, cowboy hat high on his brow, studying, ready to work, still thinking about Gabi. Nothing he could do about her. Work he could handle though.

"I'll have that all downed by lunch," he said. "Count 'em."

"Five hours?" Wilson said. "No way."

"Dallas says five hours, it's five hours," said Jimmy. "I'll put money on it."

Dallas laced up his Wesco boots, strapped on his Bashlin hooks, threw his belt over his shoulder, and picked-up his chainsaw and fuel canister. Then he hiked out.

Ten minutes later, Dallas was halfway up a tree.

He calculated where it would go, the direction and speed. He knew every danger.

He setup low, without cleaning the top. He thought the risk was minimal, but if he was wrong, he'd surely die.

Dallas gritted his teeth while the chainsaw screamed.

The tree quivered, cracking and splintering as it broke apart.

Dallas revved the chainsaw as fast as it would go. He still had three inches. If he couldn't make the cut clean, he'd be in serious trouble.

A cloud of black smoke spit out. The sound was deafening.

The saw barely made it through just in time. Dallas covered his eyes with his forearm, yelling.

The top came down in slow motion, just as Dallas had calculated, bagging and scrapping the branches as it went.

Dallas leaned back, sunk his hooks deep into the truck, as deep as they'd go, while keeping the strap of his belt taut.

When the trunk stopped quivering, Dallas climbed up and took a seat atop, and stared-out over the endless forest, into the horizon.

"Dallas, you have a phone call. Dallas, you have a phone call," he heard over the intercom.

He smiled, knowing who it was.

He climbed down the tree as fast as possible, and then he dropped his equipment at the base and stretched for just a second.

"Ain't gonna happen in five hours," he heard Wilson yell.

Dallas shrugged and jogged to the office.

"Don't hang up," he yelled when he entered.

"Been getting a lot of calls for you, Dal," said the secretary.

"Yeah. Yeah." Dallas grinned. "Here, just give me the phone."

"Hi," said Gabi.

"Been calling often?"

"Just wanted to see if you were in," she said.

"Gabi?"

"Yes?"

"We have to meet."

"Finally. It took you long enough," she said.

"You want to meet this weekend?"

"Where?"

"Halfway? he said.

"Where are you now?" she asked.

43

"Missouri."

"So, where do you want to meet?" She sounded as if she were having a hard time breathing.

"How about Springfield, Illinois?"

"Okay."

"Don't wear pants. Wear a skirt."

"Don't tell me..." she began angrily. Then, she paused. "Okay, I'll wear a skirt."

—11

DALLAS PARKED his bucket truck and walked into the hotel.

"Room for two. One bed, please."

"Driver license, and fill this out," said the clerk.

"Yes ma'am."

Dallas paid for one night.

"Where's the room?" he asked.

"Go down the hall. First left, go halfway down. It'll be on the right."

"Thanks."

Dallas's feet glided over the carpet as things began to slow down.

He went into the room, set two bottles of water on the dresser, sat on the bed, and opened the nightstand drawer.

There was a bible staring back at him.

Dallas took a deep breath, closed the drawer, and looked out the window.

The haze from the sun, hiding behind the clouds barely made it into the room.

He was early by two hours. He'd been waiting all week for this, and now he was here. He stayed in the room for one hour, pacing, staring at the walls, in the mirror, and then out the window.

He took Charles Dickens' *A Tale of Two Cities* from a plastic Wal-Mart bag. Then he went to the lobby and sat in a padded chair. He opened the book, read two pages, but stopped.

He was too nervous. He just sat there, staring, wondering.

Often, we know the crucial moments in our lives as they happen. We may not know why, what, or how they'll end or affect us throughout our lives, but we know they're happening. Memories are forged. Time becomes hard, unbendable, a needle into numb flesh.

Dallas turned, stared out the window into the parking lot.

A car pulled in, and a man got out. The car drove away. The man walked to a gas station next to the hotel.

A truck drove in and went to the back.

Dallas bit his lip.

He sat in the chair, glancing, imagining. Ideas danced in his head without rhyme or reason.

Each car brought fresh hope, only to be dashed. Elderly women, families, working men.

Then a dark sedan pulled-in and parked near the entrance.

A woman wearing a black skirt got out.

She was gorgeous. When he was a child, he dreamed he would marry a dark Latina with black wavy hair. She was his dream.

She was nervous, walking as if unsure of herself, but fast as if with purpose.

Dallas crossed himself while she looked the other way.

He stood.

As the woman walked through the first set of doors, she looked up, staring directly into Dallas's eyes. Then, she turned away.

Then, there she was, standing before him, smiling. Her dark Portuguese eyes said one word: love. It was there, pure and true.

"Hi," she said.

"Hello."

They just stood, staring at each other.

"Want to go to the room?" he asked.

A worried look overtook Gabi. She shook her head. "No."

Dallas thought about it, and then, he extended his hand.

"Want to go for a walk?" he asked.

"Okay," she said, placing her hand inside his. They turned together and walked in front of the clerk and then down the hallway.

Dallas kept glancing at Gabi. Each time he looked, she took a deep breath and smiled back.

He couldn't believe her, with her happiness clear as day. He felt the same.

He pointed down the first hallway, "Here?"

"Okay," she said.

They turned and walked deeper into the interior of the hotel, out of the daylight and into the shadows.

Halfway down, Dallas stopped and turned to face her. She looked up. Dallas stared in Gabi's eyes. He wrapped his arms around her waist, pulled her to him, and kissed her without warning.

He took hold of her body. His hands engulfed and tightened, pressing her against him.

He let go and turned to his left. Then he took out his door card and slid it through the card-reader. The light turned green. He opened the door.

He looked at Gabi and nodded to the room.

"Let's go inside?" he said.

"Okay."

Dallas took Gabi's hand and pulled her into the room.

She stared at this man she'd only seen for the first time two minutes ago.

She stood in the middle of the room, glancing, wondering. Then their eyes met again.

His right hand went between her legs. His left around her neck, pulling her hair back.

He pushed her against the bed. She sat halfway on, her legs still on the floor. He squeezed his hands between her thighs, grabbing over her skirt.

Her legs shuffled. She cried out, "Oh my God. Oh my God."

Dallas stopped, "Are you okay?"

"Yes. Oh my God." She laughed. I didn't even take my clothes off."

Dallas laughed too.

He pulled away. "Hold on," he said. "There's something I have to tell you."

"Okay," said Gabi.

"You have to know this, before we start. I will never divorce my wife or leave my family. You have to know that, okay?"

She took a deep breath. "Okay," she said.

Dallas reached out. They met and kissed passionately, hands searching, grabbing, pulling. They couldn't get their clothes off fast enough.

Gabi gasped for air, "This is so strong."

~   ~   ~

Two hours later, Dallas was above her, dripping sweat, breathing heavily. He looked down, and their eyes met. Each time he looked at her, he saw her soul elevate. She took a deep breath and smiled.

"You're sweating so much, Dallas."

"Sorry."

She reached up, ran her fingers and then her entire hand along his body, his chest, never taking her eyes from him, studying her own movement.

She put her now-wet hand over her own chest, along her body. Then she put her finger on her chin, leaving his sweat there. She put her finger against her nose.

"I love your smell," she said.

She wrapped her arms around Dallas, pulled herself up to him, put her nose against his body, and breathed in.

"What do you love?" he asked.

"God, I love all of you—your smell."

Dallas fell to his side. He couldn't go on, pulling her to him, holding her tight, running his hands through her jet-black hair.

Her nose was against his armpit, breathing him in.

Dallas got emotional. He couldn't believe this woman and the energy between them. It couldn't be real.

Finally, they talked. Gabi told Dallas her husband was a mixed martial artist and could probably hold his own against Dallas.

Dallas laughed. "I don't fight. I'd never fight your husband."

"Well, you might have to." she said, laughing.

"I stabbed a man before," said Dallas. "Down in Latin America, when I was a teenager."

"Did he die?" she asked.

Dallas shook his head and kissed her.

They made love for twelve hours, as storms pounded the bedroom window. They never left the room, only stopping for short breaks to drink water, to refresh themselves, to dream. Now, they could do anything they always wanted to. Each was free, with someone they trusted. They could do and say anything, and they did.

—12

ON HIS WAY back to his hotel near Saint Louis, Dallas pulled his truck to the side of the road.

Then he collapsed on the seat and slept. Two hours later, he awoke to a realization. Gabi's husband was cheating on her.

She wasn't the type of woman who cheated. She despised lies. She was devoted, and if she had a child, as Dallas did, she wouldn't cheat.

He took a deep breath and looked around as cars sped by. He cranked the motor to his truck and wondered what the dream, the realization, meant. Then he drove the rest of the way back to Saint Louis.

Over the next two weeks, Gabi and Dallas talked every night. She would call him as she walked into her apartment. Then, she would lie down on the sofa and masturbate, repeating his name over and over again.

They often spoke Portuguese, joking around. Dallas acted like a male chauvinist Latino, demanding that she do things, and then laughing at himself.

Gabi laughed too.

There was more confidence, more purpose, a deeper realization that what they gave would be received and returned.

They couldn't believe what was happening, the simple fact that a dream was coming true. They understood the same things, having lived between two countries, Brazil and the US. Neither fit-in anywhere, but they fit together.

They planned to meet again. The time apart was endless. Seconds, minutes, hours, days. All the clocks in the world became a cruel joke, some inventor concocted just to inflict pain.

Dallas's work, and life fell apart. He almost died twice while working seventy feet in the air, miscalculating everything. His truck caught on fire driving down Highway 255, just east of Wood River, Illinois, when he saw but refused to fix a leaky oil line.

Firemen were called and found Dallas crawling under the truck with an outdated fire extinguisher. Dallas broke the cap and was throwing the powder on the flames.

The fire chief took pity on him after Dallas broke down, in a fury, hitting the front of his truck over and over with a bloody fist.

Dallas's confidence was gone, his legs wobbly. He sweat and trembled in fear and was unable to do the simplest of tasks. His eyes gave his emotions away. So, he didn't look people in their eyes.

He also stopped talking to his wife back in Brazil. He gave up any hope of reciprocal love from her.

I just have to make it to Saturday, he thought.

As if the world would end in a few more days. No more worries, no more anything. Nothing mattered, just Saturday, *just make it to Saturday. That's all I have to do.*

—13

THIS TIME the hotel clerk knew to give Dallas a room – far off – as far from other guests as possible. Nobody wanted to hear screams and cries all day and night.

As before, Dallas sat, waiting in the same chair, pretending to read the same book.

Hours later, he held Gabi in his arms.

"How many women have you been with?" she asked.

"Not many."

"Yeah, right."

"No. It's true. What happened between us—this is the first time," he said.

"You're a liar

"Okay, I'll tell you what you want to hear if that's what you want."

"The truth. Yes. Tell me."

"You don't want the truth," he said.

"I'll know it when I hear it."

"Okay. I've had so many women."

"I know you have." Gabi laughed.

"No, Gabi. In reality, I haven't."

Gabi just kept laughing. "Look what you did to me."

"You don't believe me?" he asked.

"No, I don't. You're a lying womanizer."

"I've never done anything like this before," he said.

"Liar. Liar."

"No, I'm serious."

"How many women have you been with?" asked Gabi.

"Four. Well there was something that happened when I was twelve."

"You're such a liar."

"That's the truth. I never wanted to be with a lot of women. Never. I always wanted to find one woman and spend my life with her, live life together with one woman. That's it."

Gabi laughed. "Yeah, right. You're so full of crap."

"All right. You want to hear it?" he asked.

"Yes."

"I've slept with so many women I can't keep track."

"Now, that's the truth."

"You want to know my next conquest?"

"Yes. No. Maybe. What?" Gabi smiled.

"Your sister."

Gabi's eyes never left his.

"I'm gonna get your sister. Is that okay with you?" Dallas grinned.

"No. It's not." Gabi got serious, but she couldn't help but smile.

"Come on. I want to sleep with your sister, please?" he said.

"No, of course not."

"Oh, come on. I said please."

"No."

"Well, I'm going to anyway."

"No. You can't."

"It's no big deal, just a little fuck. Nothing like what I did to you. Okay?"

"No. I said, No. What's a little fuck anyway?"

"I grab her in the kitchen, and we hide in the closet and do it really quick. That's a little fuck."

"Oh my God. That's terrible."

Now, they were both laughing. "You are terrible," she said.

"You love this, don't you? You know I'm lying. I don't want to have anything to do with your sister." he said.

"Oh, no?"

He stared into Gabi's eyes.

"Well, I don't know. Maybe. Not really. But you like that nasty stuff. You act like you don't, but you do."

"Oh, you are terrible," she said again.

"You know, I'm not like that."

"Oh, yes you are. How many women have you really slept with – for real?"

"All right," he said. "About eighty-seven."

"I knew it. You know the exact number. I can't believe it."

Dallas kissed Gabi, and held her there. Then, he sat up, got on all fours, and began sniffing the air.

"What are you doing now?" she asked.

Dallas barked.

"Oh, now you're a dog?"

His eyes grew large.

"Arf. Arf."

He sniffed Gabi's head, licking her face, then down to her chest, licking all over. Then he lifted his hind leg.

"Oh no. Stop. Don't pee."

Dallas stopped and stared at Gabi as if trying to understand something.

"Oh my. You're crazy."

Dallas flared his nose, spun around, searching. He smelled something.

"Oh no. Stop doggy," she shouted. "Down. Sit."

Dallas' frantically searched Gabi's body for a smell. Heavy breaths and licking.

"Oh no. Oh, help me. Crazy dog."

Gabi tried to turn over. Dallas danced, throwing his paws out, growling, biting the air, barking over and over.

"Oh no. Someone, help me. There's a rabid dog in here. Help. Help."

Dallas put his face right up to Gabi's—nose-to-nose, eye-to-eye. He growled, ready to bite her.

"Okay. Okay. I'll be still. Calm doggy."

Dallas licked her face. Then he went back to sniffing the air. Then he sniffed her body, her chest, her abdomen, her waist.

"Help, help," she whispered, her hands covering her face.

The closer he got, the more frantically he sniffed.

All Gabi could do was lie still. Then, he found it.

Dallas howled.

Gabi moaned.

Five minutes later there was a knock on the door.

"Keep it down in there. We have other guests."

—14

"COME ON – let's go out."

Gabi put-on Dallas's sweaty T-shirt with nothing underneath.

Dallas walked-up to her, grabbed the bottom of his shirt, and pulled it up and down, stretching it over her nipples, watching them grow and harden, staring into her eyes, his grin widening.

"You know what'll happen if we get married?"

"What?" She was breathing heavily again.

"We'll have dinner dates with friends. We're supposed to be there at five or something like that. We'll get all dressed up. You'll get your makeup on. I'll be wearing a suit. Then, I'll grab you, kiss you. I'll do this to you."

He rubbed the shirt harder over her nipples.

They both smiled that smile that said love. It was undeniable.

"We'll strip down naked and fuck for hours. We'll show-up so late. We'll be lucky to make it by seven or eight if we make it at all. We'll be calling and cancelling all the time. We'll probably end up without friends."

"That's fine with me," she said.

"Me too. Fuck everyone."

And they stripped down naked again and made love, as if they'd each traversed an endless desert alone and just found each other.

An hour later, at two in the morning, they rose from the bed—sweaty and wobbly—and got dressed again.

She wore his shirt. He wore jeans with no underwear, a jacket, no socks, just lineman's boots.

They walked out of the hotel holding hands, stepping onto the pavement the rain had left shiny and wet.

"Every time we get together, it rains," said Gabi.

"Yeah," he said.

"We haven't even eaten together. We know nothing about each other. You know that?"

"Yeah, I know," he said.

Dallas unlocked the passenger door and opened it for Gabi. She got inside and immediately scooted over and unlocked the driver door.

Dallas got in, his eyes never leaving her, studying her up and down. "You know, you passed my mom's test," he said.

"What do you mean?"

"You unlocked my door. Mom told me to never date a woman who doesn't unlock your door the first time you get in a car with her."

"She did?"

"Yes. She said, 'If she doesn't unlock it, run.'" Dallas was serious.

"Well, that's not a big deal."

"My wife didn't do it. And when I mentioned it to her, just as I just did to you, she shrugged it off and laughed at me."

Dallas started the truck and drove around Springfield Lake. Gabi curled up at his side, his right hand covering her body, resting on her butt.

"Do you want to go up in the air?"

Gabi looked at him.

There's the smile.

"What? Go up in the air?" she said.

"Yeah, use the boom. Go up in the air?"

"Yes," she said.

Dallas pulled the truck off the road, turned on the hydraulic pump, and left the motor running. They walked to the back and climbed up into the bucket, no harness or any safety gear, and Dallas boomed straight-up, into the darkness of night.

"Look the moon." He pointed.

It was barely visible behind the clouds.

"Are you scared?" he asked her.

"No," said Gabi. "Are you?"

"A little. The height doesn't bother me. It's the night."

Gabi smiled.

"We can sit down?"

"No," said Gabi.

Dallas watched Gabi as she stood beside him, smiling with maternal eyes.

"I want you to know something," he said.

"What?"

"Whatever happens…I don't know what's going to happen, you know?"

"What do you mean?" Gabi stared at him.

"I mean, no matter what happens in the future, I want you to know, one day I'll come back into your life, and I'll do everything I can to make you mine again."

Gabi gave him a puzzled look. Then, she said, "Promise?"

"I swear to God I will," he told her.

"Why did you say that?" she asked.

"Because I want you to know that."

"That's a weird thing to say." She shivered. "I'm scared Dallas."

"Why?"

"Whenever you love someone more than you love yourself, it's always tragic."

Dallas took hold of her.

"But if you come back or something..."

"What?"

"I'm just saying, I can be very cold," she said.

"Yeah. I know. I saw that."

"No. You haven't seen anything, Dallas..."

"Yeah. I saw it."

"Well, just because you come back into my life doesn't mean I'll take you back or feel something for you. One of my old boyfriends tried that. I felt nothing for him. I just stared at him and laughed. There was no emotion. I felt nothing. I'm telling you, I can be very cold."

"Well, if I come back into your life, I'll make sure you feel something."

"Oh, how are you going to do that?" she asked.

"I don't know. But you already agreed. It's too late now," he said.

"Oh, it is?" she asked.

"Yes, it is."

Gabi laughed.

"You said, 'Promise,'" he told her.

"Yes, I did."

"So, there you go. No matter what, I'll come back into your life, and nothing will stop me."

"Well, I might not feel anything for you..."

"And you might lie to yourself," he said.

"Oh?"

They stared at each other and then out into the overcast night. The clouds sped by them in the moonlight.

Dallas pulled Gabi close. She lowered her head and let him hold her.

They held each other tightly, thirty feet in air, in the misty moonlight.

"Come on," he said. "Let's go back to the hotel. I think it's going to rain again."

—15

IN THE MORNING, Gabi lay in bed, sleeping. Sheets covered her torso.

Dallas sat in a chair, studying everything. Her soft breath, arms bent, fingers curled, angelic, as if in prayer.

He got up, slowly pulled the sheet open, and lay beside her, careful not to wake her.

Gabi's eyes opened. They stared at each other.

"How long have you been watching me?" she asked.

There it is – her smile.

Dallas smiled back and didn't say a word.

Gabi got out of bed. Dallas turned around to watch.

She drank water, went into the bathroom, and took a seat on the toilet.

Dallas followed her.

"You like to watch me, don't you?" she said.

"Yes. You're poetry, Gabi."

"Wow. So, you know poetry?"

"Oh yeah. I'm staring at it."

"Well, I guess I'm getting the whole package then, a man, a poet…" Gabi laughed.

There she was, smiling, sitting there. Then, Gabi frowned, but didn't say anything.

He stood directly in front of her, naked.

She looked up. Their eyes met.

"What is this thing in front of me?"

He smiled. They both laughed.

Just then, a sound came from the bedroom. "The legends of country music."

"What's that?" asked Gabi.

"I don't know."

Dallas walked out and looked around.

It was the clock radio.

"Someone set the alarm and didn't turn it off."

"And now, ladies and gentlemen, George Jones."

The melody began.

Dallas hummed, "I love this song. Come on."

George Jones sang, "You know this old world is full of singers, but just a few are chosen to tear your hearts out when they siiinnnnnng…"

Dallas turned up the radio, but there was too much static, so he turned it back down.

"Come here, Gabi."

She stepped out.

There's her smile.

They embraced, pressed their bodies together, stepping back and forth.

George Jones sang about radio heroes, wondering who would fill their shoes.

Dallas leaned over, farther and farther.

"We're going to fall Dallas. Stop!"

They fell over, Gabi on top.

Dallas rolled around, pinning Gabi's arms down.

"Try to escape me," he said.

"No. I don't want to."

Dallas covered his eyes. "There's nothing anyone can do anymore. It's my fault – mine – mine." Dallas peeked through his fingers.

"What's that?" she asked.

"That's my Eli Wallach impersonation."

"Who's that?"

"Nothing. Never mind." He laughed.

"Dallas, I wonder if we'd be good married."

Dallas stared blankly, and she said, "I'm just something you fuck, aren't I?"

Dallas shook his head. "If you only knew."

"You tell your friends at work you're fucking a married woman?"

Dallas laughed.

"Oh my God, you did. How could you do that?"

"No, I didn't." he said.

"Yes, you did. And I just proved that you're a liar."

"Oh my."

They lay there on the floor.

"Do you think we'd be a good husband and wife?" she asked. "Wonder what our children would look like?" She stared at Dallas. "I am a little dark."

"Don't know. I think they'd be beautiful. Your dark skin. My eyes."

"You think?" she asked.

"I want to have a baby with you, Gabi. How's that?" he said.

Gabi smiled. "I love you, Dallas."

"I love you, Gabi."

"I think if we were married, we'd be just like the others," she said.

"Would that be so bad?" He opened her legs.

"Ouch. Ouch."

"Hold on. Just the thing. Doctor's request."

"Oh no. What's that?" Gabi laughed.

"What we need right now."

"What do we need?" she asked.

"I want to see you cry," he said.

"No," said Gabi.

"Cry for me."

Gabi began to whimper. "I can't just cry, you know."

"Yes, you can."

—16

DALLAS SAT in his thirty-dollar hotel room, somewhere south of Saint Louis, near De Soto, Missouri.

He flipped through the channels, then paused when he recognized Pepé Le Pew. The mischievous skunk was talking to himself while chasing his prey, that poor little feline with a white stripe accidentally painted down her back.

"Poor old Pepé, just looking for love," said Dallas.

He clicked off the TV and put down the remote.

Just then his phone rang, and when he answered, Gabi said, "Hi."

"I can't stop thinking about you," he told her. "Couldn't work."

"Oh, I work. I have to. I don't have a choice," she said.

"Yeah."

"Well, I had to call. I ate lunch at home today, but I have to get back to work. I'm falling behind," she said.

"Thought work was going well?"

"Yeah, but not perfect."

"Gabi?"

"Yes?"

"I love you," he said.

"God, I love you too."

Gabi held the phone to her chest.

"Gabi?"

There was nothing.

"You there? Hello," he said.

Gabi closed her eyes and felt the sounds of his voice against her breast.

"Hello. Gabi? Did you hang up? Geez."

Gabi took short, deep breaths.

"I guess so."

Dallas hung up the phone.

Just then, Gabi's phone rang again.

Gabi answered it.

"G. I'm home. Let me in, honey."

Oh my God. Deep breath, deep breath.

"You there, G?"

"Yes. You don't have a key, do you?" she asked.

"No. I left it with you."

"I'm on my way, Trevor. Wait a sec."

Gabi wiped the tears from her face, looked in the mirror, took a deep breath, and walked out of the apartment.

~　　　~　　　~

Dallas stared at the phone, picked it up, and dialed.

Gabi's phone rang and rang.

Dallas hung up, packed his things, walked out of the hotel, and threw his duffle bag in the back of a taxi.

"Saint Louis International Airport," he told the driver.

—17

THE NEXT DAY, Gabi sat in her car, waiting for an order of fries and iced tea.

She turned on the radio, switching stations, up and down the dial.

"Classic country. Home of the legends."

The station went to a commercial break.

She got her order and tried the fries. *Needs ketchup, but I can't make a mess in the car.*

She took a drink, steered out of the driveway into the parking lot, listening and waiting.

"Ole Willie ladies and gentlemen – a little blue eyes…"

The melody began. *Blue Eyes Crying In the Rain.*

She couldn't take it anymore.

Gabi moaned in agony.

Traffic stopped. Her head bowed.

"Dallas."

Willie kept singing.

"No." She banged the radio, turning it off.

"I love you. God, I love you Dallas." she screamed at the top of her lungs.

A minute passed, and she calmed down, but standing still in traffic.

She reached over and turned on the radio, turning the nob as fast as possible, past the country music, back to her usual station.

Gerry Rafferty played. The symbols chimed, and the sax screamed.

She turned off the radio. "I have to stop. This is ridiculous."

She could barely breathe.

"Go cars. Go. Go."

Still, nothing moved.

"I have to stop this."

She turned the radio back on.

"I can take it."

Gerry sang. She broke down crying.

She banged the radio once again, turning it off.

Her thoughts drifted to a place of rational thought. To be a true lover, you must believe in something greater than self. Gabi was ready to surrender, just like her faith in God. Yes. She was willing to leap-off into the unknown for God, Jesus, her faith, to create and have the ultimate love. Nothing else was worthy of her life.

In other words, she believed.

Gabi turned the radio back on and listened to her music, telling herself it was going to work out.

—18

WHEN DALLAS ARRIVED in São Paulo, he left the airport and jumped in a taxi.

He got Gabi's childhood home address and directions from her before he left. He had to see where she grew up, to understand her.

It didn't matter that he missed his flight to his final destination and would have to purchase another ticket.

He took a taxi to the closest Metro, the Red Line, and took it to the Tatuapé Metro station, where he got out and followed Gabi's instructions.

He walked a block from the Metro, turned right, and found himself in front of a large, gated, two-story home across from a large apartment building.

He remembered Gabi talking about the time her mother found out she lost her virginity when she caught Gabi with condoms in her backpack. She was fourteen. "The fight was terrible," she said.

Dallas laughed, telling her, he beat her by two years. Gabi laughed too.

They didn't mind sharing these embarrassing facts. That was life. Full of troubles, heartbreak, and stupidity.

Dallas didn't mind when she told him about her first American boyfriend who lived in the apartment building in front of her home. She would look out her window and watch him.

Dallas stood there in front of her house. He saw the girl that Gabi was—her long, flowing, wavy black hair, the Catholic skirt she wore to school, her smiles, her tears. She ran up and down the street, got into fights with her brother and sister. There were struggles, insanity, which is common in São Paulo, a place where he'd also lived and felt a strong connection.

Dallas knelt and then sat on the curb. He stayed there for an hour, dreaming, realizing. He knew this woman was connected to him in so many ways.

—19

OUT THE WINDOW he viewed green pastels, millions of shades – layered – one atop the other. Color, he thought. Vibrancy.

The plane landed in Curitiba. Some passengers got off, and some got on. The plane took off again, and an hour later, it landed in Londrina.

Dallas walked off the plane, hoping to find his wife and son, whom he hadn't seen in over a year.

There was no one.

He got his bags, walked out of the airport, and stood alone, as the many passengers hugged and kissed family members.

After he had waited more than two hours, a Ford pick-up stopped. A woman got out. Joy! Finally.

"Come-on hurry. Get in," she shouted.

"You know how long I've been waiting?" he said. "Aren't you happy to see me? Come on. Give me a hug."

"We don't have much time." Joy gave him a dutiful hug. "Hurry, get inside." She returned to the driver's seat.

"No. No. I'm driving," he said.

"No, you don't know how to drive this."

"Why do you think that?" he asked.

"It's a stick-shift," she said.

"Are you kidding me? You think I can't drive a stick-shift.

"I never saw you drive one."

"You have no faith in your husband," he said. "I bought and paid for this truck, and you think I can't drive it? Well, I'm going to."

"Oh, you're such an asshole, Dallas."

"Yeah, I'm an asshole, right? What took you so long? We haven't seen each other in a year. You can't even get to the airport on time and pick me up. Where's my son?"

"Oh, stop complaining," she said. "There are things that have to get done. The farm."

"No shit."

I bought and paid for the farm, but I don't know anything, he thought.

Dallas pressed the clutch in and put it in second.

"You just put it in second, idiot." said Joy.

Dallas released the clutch. The truck pulled forward. He got it up to thirty and then shifted to third.

"First is a granny gear," he said.

"Oh, what's that?" she asked. "You think you know everything."

—20

"*WHERE'S MY BOY?*"

"He's in his room," said Joy.

Joy stood in Dallas' path in the middle of the hallway.

Dallas looked from side to side, out the kitchen window, at the view, the trees, and now back to her. He could already sense the pressure building in her.

"What are you lookin' at?" Joy just stood there. "Now, you tell me the truth," she said.

He took a deep breath. "What?"

"Dallas, did you cheat on me?"

"What the hell question is that?"

"I want to know – right now." she demanded.

"I can't believe you'd ask that," he said. "We haven't seen each other in a year. I just get home. I haven't even seen my son. And that's what you ask me?"

"Did you? Tell me. You did, didn't you?"

Dallas stared and shook his head.

"Let me see Aaron." He shook his head. "Can't believe you asked me that."

"Dallas." Joy didn't move. "Did you?"

"Stop this questioning."

"I want to know, Dallas."

"Okay. But that's the first thing you ask me when I get home?"

"Tell me."

"Yes. I did."

Joy slapped Dallas across the face as hard as she could.

"You fucking asshole." Her hand recoiled, ready to strike again.

"Stop this shit." Dallas backed away.

She advanced.

"You're a piece of shit, Dallas. I'm home taking care of everything. You're out there, cheating on me."

"What do you want from me?" He didn't know what to say. This isn't what he wanted to come home to.

"I hate you, you piece of shit." Joy continued to scream, tears in her eyes. "How could you do that to me?"

Dallas just stared at her.

—21

LATE AT NIGHT, Dallas and Joy lay in bed, getting ready to sleep.

"Now. Let me ask you a question," Dallas said.

"What?"

"Remember – this was a few years ago – three years ago, you were calling your old boyfriend, James, almost every day. And then you flew back to Boston. Remember?"

"Yes."

"You spent Christmas with Mara, your friend. Did you sleep with your old boyfriend?"

"No." said Joy.

"You didn't?"

"Don't try to turn things around, Dallas. You always do this. You manipulate people. I swear to God I didn't sleep with him."

"You swear to God?" he asked.

"Yes. I swear to God."

Dallas sat up, his eyes searching the dark room.

"But you were talking with him every day for nearly a month. Did you see him when you went back?"

"You always do this. You cheated on me. You did it. Now you want to blame me. How could you cheat on me, Dallas? We're married. How could you do it?"

"Okay. All right."

"Dallas." Joy stared nodding. "You really are a piece of shit."

"Okay. Okay. Let's do this," he said. "There're things that turn you on, right? Tell me. We'll do them. Whatever you want. I don't care. Let's just have fun in bed, okay?"

"I'm not interested," she said. "There's no attraction."

"I know. I know."

"You don't understand," she said.

"No. Stop. Listen. I'm willing to do or talk about whatever turns you on. I don't care what it is, some strange sexual thing, just tell me. I'm your husband. Just tell me something that turns you on."

"What are you saying, that we don't have sex?"

"No. I'm saying, let's have some fun, do something stupid, whatever."

"No. You're saying we don't have sex." Joy crossed her arms over her chest.

"No. I'm saying we should have some fun."

"Dallas, we have sex all the time."

"Barely, and when we do, it's boring."

"We have sex."

"When?"

"Fuck you," she screamed.

"Do you want me to force you? What do you want? Let me in. Damn." Dallas pulled her close, kissing her.

"Stop. Stop. I don't want this."

Joy fought, her arms pushing Dallas away.

"Come on," said Dallas.

"Stop it, Dallas."

"Is it really that bad?"

"It's terrible," she said.

77

"Look at you breathing so hard. Let's do it while we're excited. Let's just go with it."

"We should get a divorce," she said. "We should've never gotten married. I fucking hate you. I hate you. You're evil." She started to sob.

Dallas sat up, looked out the window, and sighed.

"You know, you've said that to me since we got married," he said. "'We should've never gotten married. We should get a divorce.' I've heard you say that, I can't count how many times. Okay, then. Let's get a divorce. You can call me the bad guy if you want. I'm just as tired of this as you are. I don't even care anymore. Let's just get a divorce, and I'm going to be with this other woman. Done."

Dallas got up from the bed and turned on the stereo.

Joy stared at him. Her eyes narrowed.

The song on the radio was Skank's, *Eu Disse a Ela – I told her*.

Dallas sang along.

—22

DALLAS SPENT HIS days working on the farm, that he had bought for his in-laws.

He wasn't a rancher or a farmer. He didn't ride horses. He didn't drive a tractor. He knew nothing, but that was okay. He simply asked his father-in-law what to do and how to do it. He was happy to be in the fields – working. He picked up equipment, moved pumps and hoses for irrigation, fertilized and sprayed corn, barbecued and swam in the river that surrounded his land.

At night, he'd return to his apartment in downtown Apucarana, avoid Joy, shower, and then sit in the kitchen and wait for Gabi's phone call.

But, for the past week, she hadn't called.

Gabi said she couldn't go on. The guilt of her infidelity was too much. Dallas understood, but he still waited, believing one day she would pick up the phone and dial his number.

Then one night, she did.

It was ten o'clock. The phone rang twice.

"Hello. Gabi," he said, heart pounding.

"Hi."

"Oh God. Thank you for calling."

"You didn't give up on me?" she asked.

"Never."

"You forgive me?" she said.

"Always," he said.

"Oh my God...Dallas." Gabi cried. "My husband knows everything. I said your name in my sleep, over and over, and I had to tell him. He called me every name in the book, and then, he admitted he cheated on me."

"What if he didn't cheat on you, Gabi?"

"I don't know. I don't want to think about that."

"So, now what?" he asked.

"I just want to be with you, Dallas."

"God, I want to be with you too."

"Give your wife the farm and come back to the US. Or do you want me to go back to Brazil? For you, I will."

"You have to come down to Brazil," he said. "And we can spend our birthdays together. They're only three days apart."

"Okay." He could hear the excitement in her voice. "We can meet in São Paulo, okay?"

"Okay. Let's do it."

"If you can't make it, I'll go to Apucarana, okay? So, let me know. I'll go there."

"No. I'm going to make it," he said.

"When we meet..." Her voice broke. "... let's never separate again, okay?"

"Yes." Of course, he thought. He should have known they belonged together.

"I can't take this again." She sobbed. "We should've never left each other."

"Oh, Gabi, I know."

They talked until the sun came up, and he felt a calmness between them, a confidence, and an understanding. Even the most terrible things they'd ever done or would do to each other would be forgiven, no matter what. Everything would be okay between them. Each would always understand the other.

With Dallas still on the phone, Gabi began to make breakfast.

"Oh my God. I got to go. My husband just woke up. Bye. I love you."

Trevor entered the kitchen. "Who were you on the phone with?" he asked.

Gabi stared at her husband and felt herself flush. Let him guess. She wasn't going to say a word.

Trevor was always calculating. His brown eyes at the same level of Gabi's, held steady, but they figured things out. Ever degree, action, reaction, was worked out before a movement. Heaven forbid the outcome wasn't correct.

"Let me tell you something, bitch," he said. "She was gorgeous. And I wasn't with a married woman."

"Yeah, so where is she now, Mr. Don Juan?"

"Back at school," said Trevor.

"At least, with Dallas I have something real," she said. "It's special. I love him, and he loves me."

"That dude is just using you," Trevor said. "He doesn't care about you."

"He loves me. I know."

"He doesn't love you. You're just another notch on his belt."

"You held what I did over me," Gabi said, "lying to me about what you did."

"What's the big deal about this asshole?" Trevor's jaw was set, and she knew she was in for a shouting match.

"We fit together," she said, no longer caring about Trevor's rage.

Instead he went quiet and took a step toward her. "You're such a fool," he said. Then, he turned and stomped out of the kitchen.

—23

TREVOR CLOSED the door.

Gabi sat at her table and took a bite of toast.

The phone rang.

When Gabi answered, there was silence for a moment. Then a woman asked, "Is this Gabriela?"

"Yes."

"This is Dallas's wife. Joy."

Gabi nearly choked on her toast. "What do you want?"

"You know you're destroying my family. We have a child, a two-year-old son. Dallas is my husband – not yours. What type of a woman are you?"

Gabi held her hand to her mouth, feeling the tears come, unable to stop them.

"What do you think you're doing? Leave Dallas alone."

Tears poured from Gabi's eyes.

"Say something. Why my husband? Get another man." She sounded out of her mind with pain. Gabi felt terrible, but she couldn't speak.

"Say something. I deserve an answer. Tell me. Why my husband?"

"There's something…I don't know what to say…"

"Why Dallas?"

"I don't know," she sobbed. "I think we're soulmates."

"Oh, you're something else," Joy said. "But you've got to leave him alone."

Gabi felt her head shaking. "No," she said. "I love him." Joy was still swearing when Gabi ended the call.

—24

"I CAN'T STOP thinking about you. I want to take care of you. You're like a little child – so naïve. I don't care about anything else…Do you want me to move back to Brazil? I will for you."

Joy had enough. She walked through the kitchen – in front of Dallas – without looking at him.

"Hold on…" Dallas lowered the phone to his chest.

Joy pulled a chair from the breakfast nook, slid it across the floor, under the kitchen window, climbed up on the chair, stepped through the window, and out on the ledge.

"Oh my God." Dallas dropped the phone.

Joy stood-out on the ledge, against the wall, trying to keep her balance.

"Stop." Dallas panicked.

"What's going on?" asked Gabi. "Dallas, are you there?"

But Dallas was gone.

"I'm going to kill myself," Joy shouted. "I'm going to jump."

"Stop." Dallas rushed to the window. "Don't, Joy. Please."

"I will. I swear to God I will. If you leave me Dallas, that's it. I swear."

"Oh my God. Stop." Dallas reached out to her from the window.

Joy was crying, holding on to the side of the building, her hair a matted mess in the breeze.

"Look what you're doing to this family. You're a terrible father and husband. Look what you're making me do."

"Jesus."

The realization that he really was a terrible man, a terrible father, and everything he'd done was destructive…It all came home.

"God, I really am bad," he said.

Dallas reached out to Joy. She inched back, toward the window.

"Look in the next room. There's your two-year-old son. Just look at what you're doing."

Dallas stood motionless his hands still reaching for his wife.

"Look. Aaron is playing. And his mother is about to die. Look at what you're doing to this family."

That was it. Dallas was broken.

—25

"IT'S A SIN," said the priest.

Gabi knelt in the cramped, dark confession chamber. "It feels so right," she said, peeking from behind the cloth into the church.

"It isn't."

Gabi began to cry.

"I'm following my heart," she said.

"Maybe you're following your own rules, child. That's dangerous, and a sin."

"Maybe…"

"You've always been a problem child, Gabi," he said. "I discussed you with your priest in Brazil."

"What?" Now, she was angry. "I've done everything I've been asked. My husband converted for the marriage."

"I was the one who married you, he said. "Priests take vows of chastity Gabi. That doesn't mean we don't understand the heart. It means we can see clearly."

"No, you don't understand, Father."

He took a breath as if she'd knocked the air from him. "I knew what you were thinking even then, knew you'd always do this."

"Oh, Father…"

"No," the priest continued. "I know this is hard. You must do the right thing. I know all about your past, my child. Your father did the same. Shame passes down generations."

Gabi shook her head. "Please don't say this."

"You see. I know what you're thinking. Tell me."

"This is bullshit," she whispered.

"You see, child?" he smiled.

"I'll have nothing to do with the church. You're run by men who don't know about anything, and who do not care about women."

Gabi got up and walked from the confessional chamber.

She knelt and prayed at the first pew.

Then, she wiped a tear from her cheek and shook her head.

"See you Sunday, child," said the priest.

He'd been watching her. Furthermore, he was holding something that sure looked like a flask. Well, everyone knew he enjoyed a drink now and then, she thought. She'd probably driven him to it today.

"Thank you, Father."

Gabi walked down the aisle but stumbled on something and lost her balance. She tried to regain it, but slipped and fell.

A choirboy ran to her side. "Are you okay?"

"I'm fine," she said, even though she clearly was not, sitting there on the floor.

She grabbed the wooden bench beside her and lifted herself up. The choirboy tried to hold her elbow.

"Please stop."

She stood up and straightened her skirt and blouse.

Behind her, she could hear the boy talking to the priest in a hushed voice.

She looked back in time to see the priest sigh.

"And they wonder why we drink," he said.

"What, Father?" asked the boy.

"Oh nothing."

The priest looked to the line of men and women waiting, and said, "Next."

—26

WAYLON JENNINGS and Willie Nelson's *Momma, Don't Let Your Babies Grow up to be Cowboys* was playing as Dallas drove down the road, pulling a trailer loaded with farm equipment. The Perkins diesel purred.

Dallas's mind drifted. He was back in Illinois, running his fingers through Gabi's dark hair, watching her eyes, her smile. His soul lifted his worries for a brief moment. Then, he realized where he was and what he was doing. Work.

A green car in the right-hand lane was moving slowly.

Dallas changed lanes without slowing or speeding-up.

He passed the car like it was standing still.

Just when he turned on his passenger-side turn signal to move into the right lane, the car sped up.

He turned off his turn signal.

"What the…"

The two vehicles climbed a hill, side by side. Dallas gunned the accelerator, not about to lose speed.

He wanted to move back over to the slow lane, but now, the car was overtaking him.

"Okay?" Dallas stared at the green car, unable to make out the driver.

When they both made it to the top, the car was beside Dallas. Then, it passed him and moved over into his lane, proceeding to slow down.

"What?"

Dallas shifted gears, glanced back behind his trailer, punched the accelerator, and put his turn signal on, to pass the car on the right.

The small green car moved to the right lane, clearly preventing him.

"Motherfucker."

Dallas downshifted again, as the two vehicles started up another hill. The car took off, up the hill, leaving Dallas far behind.

This went on for miles as Dallas felt his frustration grow. The car slowed, preventing Dallas from passing. Then it would speed up to climb the hills.

Dallas cussed and screamed. A quarter mile off was an intersection. The light was green.

"I know what you're gonna do, motherfucker," Dallas said aloud, "and I don't even give a shit."

The green car slowed and then slowed more. Dallas didn't even try to pass.

"Go ahead, bitches," he said.

Now, he could see what looked like a bunch of college students inside, pointing and laughing, waving at him.

"Go ahead. Think this is my first rodeo?"

The light turned yellow. The car was crawling and then, it sped up. Dallas was left far behind but stomped on the accelerator, revving the engine. His truck barely moved, but it did gain speed.

Finally, the light turned red, and the car entered the intersection. The college students waved goodbye to Dallas.

Cars from different directions entered the intersection. Dallas' truck and trailer came in at full speed, horn blowing.

The cars stopped as the truck flew through the intersection.

Dallas was laughing. "Now whatcha gonna do, motherfuckers?" he screamed. "There ain't no more stoplights."

Dallas got right behind the little car, honking his horn.

The car slowed. Dallas wouldn't pass.

"Go. Pull over bitches. Be fucking men," he screamed out the window. "There's four of you and one of me. What you afraid of?"

The small green car sped up, Dallas did too.

The kids were laughing – yelling – their heads spinning to look at him.

The car slowed. Dallas did too.

"Go," he yelled.

The car changed lanes, slowed, and then it sped up to about seventy. Dallas was right on their tail, flashing his lights, laughing.

Then, they slowed.

"Okay, maybe they had enough," Dallas said to himself, "I was a kid too. Let them be."

The kids were staring directly at Dallas when they saw him look the other direction. One of them popped his head out the window and screamed, "Pussy cowboy Americano."

"Okay, motherfuckers." Dallas swerved his truck directly into the small car, scrapping the entire side, smashing it off the road.

The green car lurched up an embankment.

Dallas pulled over and stopped.

"Okay, now we fight," he shouted as he exited the truck, took his hat off, threw it in the cab, and stood on the side of the road. "The fuck you doing? Get the fuck out. You think your green car is special, bitches? I'll take on all you, right now."

All four of the college students stared at Dallas.

Both the car's passenger-side tires were flat, the rims bent.

They had no idea what to do.

91

Dallas grabbed his crotch. "Get out. You got no balls, bitches. Get the fuck out."

He approached the green car.

The car wobbled off the embankment – slowly from the curb – then down the road.

"Get some of these," Dallas screamed as the car drove away, leaving Dallas still grabbing his crotch.

—27

THE PHONE RANG AND RANG – night after night – at Dallas's house, but he didn't answer.

Then, finally, a few weeks before Gabi and Dallas were supposed to meet, Dallas answered the phone.

"Dallas, oh my God, thank God you answered. What happened?"

Dallas was silent. His eyes went to the kitchen window.

"What's wrong, Dallas?" asked Gabi.

Dallas covered his eyes, wincing in pain.

"I don't know...I..."

"Yes?"

"I think I have to stop..." He bent-over with his hand over his stomach.

"Please talk to me," said Gabi.

"I've got to go."

"Are we going to meet?"

"I don't know..."

"Are you going to be there, in São Paulo?" asked Gabi.

Again, he couldn't speak. He only clutched the phone.

"No matter what, I'll be there waiting for you, Dallas. If I have to, I'll go to your home. I have to see you."

"I've got to go..."

"No. Please don't do this. What happened? Oh my God. No."
Gabi cried.

Dallas hung up the phone.

"*LISTEN TO ME,* the truth is always a compliment – even if it's insulting," said Dallas as he and Gilberto sat at the kitchen table.

"That's crazy," said Gilberto, his brother-in-law.

"This doesn't work financially," said Dallas. "We've lost a lot of money, and we're still losing."

"I don't want to hear it," said Gilberto.

"Then why take the money in the first place?"

"It's not my money, not my problem," said Gilberto.

"Exactly, that's the point," Dallas said. "It's my money."

Joy entered the room, her eyes wide, lips in a tight, bitter line. Her unfinished fingernails pounded the desk. The smell of nail polish thick in the air. "Don't tell my family what to do, Dallas."

"How's this supposed to work?" asked Dallas.

"You're here doing nothing," Gilberto told him. "I'm out in the fields."

"That's got nothing to do with it. All you have to do is follow a plan."

"Yeah, your plan, right Dallas?" Joy crossed her arms and ignored the chair Dallas pulled out for her.

"Yes. Any plan. A fucking budget. We all talk things over make a decision, and stick with it. It's called business." Dallas slapped his forehead.

"We should've never gotten married." screamed Joy.

"Don't fucking say that." At that moment, he wished they'd gone through their plans to divorce.

"Don't tell my family what to do. You're not their boss."

"Someone has to. They're losing all my money." said Dallas.

"It's our money," she said.

"Okay, then act like it."

She sighed. "We should get a divorce."

"This is a fucking joke." A broken fucking record, Dallas thought.

"Fuck you and your numbers," Gilberto said, no doubt empowered by Joy's disrespect. "I don't even care."

Dallas got up from the table and threw the calculator against the wall.

"Do you have any idea how much money we lost?" he said.

"I don't care." Gilberto shrugged.

"You don't care?" asked Dallas.

"No.".

"Then why live off my money? Go get a job. Take care of yourself."

"I don't give a shit about the farm," said Gilberto.

Dallas lifted his hand in the air, ready to strike Gilberto the way he would have struck those college boys. Then he pounded it against the wall – over and over again – screaming – until his hand was bloody and shot with pain.

He walked-out of the apartment, down the stairs, out the building, across the street, and into a restaurant. He took a seat. Then, still bleeding, he ordered a soda and stared-out the window.

Joy entered the restaurant. She walked up to him and said, "You're such an asshole Dallas."

"I think my hand's broken," he said, and lifted it. "There's a bone sticking-out here,– and it's fucking painful."

"Oh my God. Look at it." Her eyes went wide. "You have to go to a hospital."

Dallas closed his eyes. Joy helped him up.

"Don't help me. I just can't drive. You drive."

"Yes. Okay." she said.

—29

GABI SAT BY the phone, in her father's apartment in São Paulo, waiting, crying, calling, waiting, and then going through the whole range of actions and emotions again.

Gabi finally broke down. Sobbing, she got up, opened a drawer, and stared at a knife. Then she picked it up – held it – staring at the sharp edge.

She slammed the draw shut.

Trevor entered the kitchen.

"Please, leave me alone. Let me be."

"Stop Gabi. Stop this." He reached out and took hold of her hand.

"Let go of the knife." He took it from her.

"God." she screamed.

"Stop this." He set the knife down on the counter.

"Get out of the way." Gabi tried to walk around him, reaching for the car keys.

"Stop, Gabi. Where you going to go?"

Her sister Gen entered the kitchen.

"Stop, Gabi," she screamed.

"Leave her alone," said Trevor. "I know how to deal with this."

"I'm going to his house, to see him." Gabi had to, regardless of what happened.

"Don't do it. Leave him alone," said Trevor.

"I want to see him. I just want to see him. I have to see him."

"He had his fun with you." Trevor chuckled, and she knew part of him was enjoying this. "He's a womanizer. Look at yourself. You won't let him go. You'll be that crazy woman chasing a married man. He just used you."

"No. That's not true." But was it? Why wasn't he here the way he promised?

"He's just trying to let you down easy, and you don't even see it," Trevor said.

"You're wrong."

Trevor took hold of her firmly. She fought against him.

"You met this guy on a hotline," he said. "How many times has he done this?"

Gabi covered her face. Trevor's arms held her tightly.

Gen shook her head and said, "Stay calm, Gabriela."

"Shut up, Genevieve," she shouted.

But she couldn't shout away the feelings, the doubts. Even as she fought against Trevor, Gabi felt her voice weaken. Dallas wasn't coming. He didn't want her now. Maybe he never really had.

Life!

The Big Stuff.

—30

AFTER LIFE BREAKS US, routines become easier, understood, manageable. You pick up a tragedy and put it here, and happiness over there. Death—there's a place for it too. Life's events become a process, things that must be done. They happen over and over again: A little joy, a little heartache. Music isn't as sweet. Glances are meaningless. A flick of the hair, crossing of legs; the act isn't important. But the result, the outcome, the sum of the equation— dry, pointless, over-analyzed, and thoroughly known.

One afternoon, Dallas heard an old song on the radio, *Only You* by the band Yazoo, and his thoughts went to Gabi. As a matter of fact, whenever he heard a love song, his thoughts went to her.

I have to send her this song.

Within some, no matter how deep the emotion is buried – under endless layers – all the years, the fear, the pain, hope grows. Like a seed so deep in the earth – no light – no water – nothing – but it won't be denied. Beyond all explanation, it sprouted.

And two years after Dallas was broken, the father, the husband, reached-out to Gabi.

He put together a package with music and a letter. He sent it to her work. Then, he called her.

After a fumbled greeting on his part, and an equally fumbled response on her part, she said, "I know why you didn't come to São Paulo."

Dallas took a deep breath, wanting to tell Gabi everything, but he didn't. Not even he understood why he didn't go to São Paulo. He just sat there and listened, unsure what to say or think.

"My husband kept telling me you were using me," she said.

"That's not it," said Dallas.

"I know it's not true. You're married and have a child. You said you wouldn't leave. I thought about killing myself," she said.

"Oh God."

Gabi giggled and then sighed.

"And the sex with your wife," she said.

"Stop."

"Don't give me that. I know sex with her is good."

"Oh no." Dallas covered his face.

"Don't lie to me," she said.

"Did you receive my package?" asked Dallas.

"Yes. I think I have to throw everything away."

Dallas sighed.

"Gabi, listen," he said.

"Go ahead…"

"I love you." he said.

There was a long pause.

"Yeah, I love you too."

"Okay?"

"Yes. Okay."

"Bye, Dallas," she said.

"Bye, Gabi."

Dallas waited for Gabi to hang up. She did.

Dallas's gaze went out the apartment window, the high rises, the tops of trees.

~   ~   ~

Gabi, played the CD that Dallas sent her. She listened to the first song, *Only You...*

After a minute, she skipped it and went to the next one, Christopher Cross's *Author's Theme.*

Gabi turned off the stereo and threw the CD in the trash.

—31

"THAT'S IT. We're bankrupt," said Dallas. "All our money – everything – gone. And we have a million dollars of debt. Banks are taking the land."

He stared at Joy, her dark eyes narrowed in thought, almost angry. She didn't look at all remorseful as she straightened out her blouse.

"If your family just would've done what I asked them." he said.

"Shut-up, Dallas. You're not their boss. I want…"

"Yeah. Yeah. I know. You want a divorce," he said.

Joy stared at Dallas. "You think you know everything."

"No."

"Yes, you do. Our entire marriage. You want to control everything – everyone."

"Yeah, right." Dallas sighed. "We lost all our money, Joy."

"Poor you," she said.

"Yeah."

"You want to tell everyone what to do, all the time." Joy waved a finger in the air as if calling on God to strike Dallas down.

"Okay," he said.

"You sit there, with that look, as if you know everything," she said. "You don't know shit."

"All right," he said. "I guess we have to start over."

"Good. I want to go back to the US."

"Yeah. I know."

So, that was that. Within six months Dallas, his wife, and son, returned to the United States.

He got his old job back in the Midwest. Found his old friends – and enemies – bought equipment, rented a mobile home in a small town, and went to work in Indiana, Southern Illinois, and eastern Missouri.

But he didn't forget.

—32

"BREATHE IN. Breathe out."

Gabi screamed in pain.

"Here she comes. Keep pushing."

Gabi took quick, short breaths.

"In – out – in – out," said Trevor.

"I know," she yelled.

"That's it," the doctor told her. "Keep going Gabi."

Her body was ripping apart. She took a tight grip of her gown, pressing, grabbing, squeezing.

"Ohhhh…" she cried.

"You're doing so good. Keep pushing," said the doctor.

Then silence. No one said a word.

A feeling of relief. Gabi's body relaxed.

"You did it," said Trevor.

The baby took one enormous gasp of air, held it in, every tiny muscle contracted, and then, she screamed.

"Oh, there," said a nurse.

"Welcome to the world," said the doctor.

"You did it, Gabi." Trevor seemed dazed. "You really did it."

Gabi glared at him but then saw her baby and smiled. Tears streamed down her face.

"Let me hold her." Gabi laughed and cried.

"You're not well," the nurse told her. "You need to stay calm."

"Let me hold her right now. Give her to me."

The nurse cut the umbilical cord and tied it.

The baby was covered in blood, still screaming.

The nurse carefully placed the baby in Gabi's hands, and the baby immediately stopped her crying.

Gabi held her, and God held Gabi. There was peace.

Here she is.

Chills went through Gabi's body. She whimpered. Tears poured. She lowered her head, brought the bloody baby to her lips, and kissed her.

"Are you okay?" asked Trevor.

"Yes. She's okay," one of the nurses said, her voice soft.

The pain, the heartache, none of it mattered now that she held her baby girl in her arms. Everything had come full circle.

Her baby made it. She was here; the joy of her life – everything. Nobody could deny her.

She lifted her gaze, not to the white-tiled ceiling, but to heaven, to God, to her mother.

"She's going to be named after you, Mom," said Gabi.

Gabi was a mother.

—33

ONE AFTERNOON – late in the day, the Illinois winter sun was low on the horizon when Aaron walked into the kitchen and set his backpack on the dining room table.

"What are you doing?" asked Joy.

"What?"

Joy held a frying pan in her hand, ready to move the meat onto a plate.

"Move it. Off the table."

Aaron scowled.

"Boy. Move it. Or else." Joy smiled at her son.

"Or else, what?" Aaron mumbled. "You touch me, I'll call the cops."

Joy put the frying pan back on the stove.

"What did you say to me?"

"The cops…" Aaron couldn't even finish the sentence. Joy slapped him across the face two times.

"Like hell you will, you little shit."

Aaron stared at her.

"Don't you dare look at me like that. I'll slap your ass again," she said. "Now, get your bag off this table."

Aaron grabbed his backpack and went to his room.

Just then, Dallas came home from work. He took off his boots, pounded the snow from his jacket, shed the layers of clothes, and then entered the kitchen. He noticed something was wrong and asked, "Where's Aaron?"

"Can you believe he said, he'd call the cops if I hit him? His own mother."

"What did you do?" asked Dallas.

"I hit him." said Joy.

"Good."

"Can you believe that?" Joy shook her head.

"Hey, Aaron," Dallas called out.

A muffled, "What?" came from the boy's room.

"Ain't gonna say that again, are you?"

"No," said Aaron.

Dallas sat in the chair, laughing. "He got that in school, you know?"

"What the hell are those schools teaching our children?" she said.

"They wonder why kids go crazy. Trying to convince them how to turn their own parents into criminals."

Dallas approached Joy and tried to hold her hand.

She pulled away.

"You think we might?" he said.

"I don't want to hear it."

"You don't even know what I'm gonna say?" said Dallas.

"Yes, I do." Joy giggled. "You stink. If you want to kiss me, go take a shower. Did you take a shower yesterday?"

Dallas mumbled as he walked away.

~   ~   ~

After dinner, Joy was on the computer, chatting with her friends in Brazil. She noticed a familiar name on the screen, on her network.

Gabriela da Silva Rogers had visited Joy's account.

Is this that Gabriela?

Joy smiled. "Dallas, come into the office."

"What's up?" he asked.

"Look." She pointed to the computer. "Let me ask you a question."

"Yeah?"

"Look at that picture. Is that the Gabriela?"

Dallas stared at the picture – the dark wavy hair, brown skin, dark Portuguese eyes, that smile.

He walked away without saying a word.

"Is that her, Dallas? Is that her?" Joy laughed.

Dallas still didn't say anything.

"Well, tell me."

"Yeah, that's her," he said.

"Look, she went on my account."

"Okay, that's fine," Dallas sat on the sofa.

"Don't you think that's weird?"

Dallas shrugged. "I don't know."

~   ~   ~

That night, Dallas couldn't sleep. He got up from his bed. Joy was sleeping in the living room, the way she usually did now because, she said, Dallas snored.

110

He walked to the kitchen and then to his son's room, watching Aaron. He ran his hand through the boy's hair, and kissed him on the forehead.

Dallas finally fell asleep about four in the morning. When he woke up two hours later, he dressed and left for work.

Dallas spent the day lost in thought, often finding himself staring into the distance, up at the white and gray clouds, wondering where Gabi was and what sky she was under.

Then, after time, as things do, the image faded away.

—34

AT WORK – DALLAS ran his chainsaw. He was nervous around the men, more so than usual.

At lunch,– Jimmy and Dallas were walking into the mess tent when he spotted Ryan at the entrance.

Ryan made a slurping noise as he drank his coffee.

"Here pussy, pussy, pussy, pussy."

Some of the guys laughed.

Dallas glanced around.

"You know you are what you eat," said Ryan.

Ryan walked closely behind Dallas. The men watched.

"Think it's 'bout time?" asked a stranger.

"Ya," said Ryan, "I do."

Men got out of the way.

Jimmy stood watching.

Dallas didn't look his way. He put his right hand up, letting Jimmy know he was alone.

"Let it go," said Jimmy.

Ryan shook his arms, stretching. Then he cracked his knuckles. He pointed to the foreman.

"This is old. Before your time."

The foreman nodded, looked around, and stepped backward.

The men formed a circle, laughing and yelling.

"Come on, Dallas." a man shouted.

"You can take him, Ryan."

"You don't stand a chance, pussy boy," said a man directly behind Dallas.

Someone pushed Dallas forward. He didn't take his eyes off Ryan though.

Ryan threw two short lefts, just testing Dallas.

Then Ryan threw a right cross at his face.

Dallas flinched, a mistake.

Bam. Ryan nailed Dallas on the chin with another right cross.

Dallas fell headfirst to the floor.

Ryan threw punches, pounding Dallas's head, bouncing it off the concrete.

"Eat that, faggot," Ryan shouted.

"It's over," Jimmy shouted back, and the other men joined in.

"It's over."

"End it."

"Pull him away."

"The asshole almost killed Ryan," another man said.

"He deserves it." said another.

"Okay," Jimmy said, "but it's over."

Men pulled Ryan away.

Dallas couldn't stand. He staggered as he got to his feet. He knew he was badly hurt, bleeding and drooling blood. He stumbled, then fell over.

Dallas didn't care. He ran at Ryan, still swinging.

Jimmy pulled him away. "Stop, Dallas."

"You want more. Tomorrow, you'll get more."

Ryan laughed. "You ain't nothing, Dallas. A fucking pushover, bitch."

The men pulled Ryan farther away.

Jimmy had a look of disgust, as he held Dallas.

"Forget about it, Dal. It's over. Come on, you're hurt. Let's go to the infirmary."

Dallas pushed him away.

"Don't let me see you around here again, Dallas," Ryan shouted.

"Fuck you, Ryan," he replied and spit blood.

~   ~   ~

An hour later, Dallas stood under a tree, his hooks on his feet, his belt around the trunk. He looked up. Blood dripped into his eyes. He shook his head and took a quivering, scared breath.

"Don't do it, Dal," said Jimmy.

Dallas began to climb, sinking his hooks deep into the truck, throwing his strap.

"Son of a bitch." Jimmy watched Dallas. "Told you to get help."

Dallas couldn't see. He slapped the side of his head, trying to shake the blood and sweat from face.

His equipment was too heavy. His body didn't respond. His mind wasn't working. Five minutes later, he was thirty feet up, completely out of breath.

He slipped and then regained his balance.

His hands, trembled.

Everything was off, wrong, uncomfortable, sweaty, out of place. Then the anger came, the frustration.

Dallas began to scream.

"Come down, Dallas." yelled Jimmy.

"I just got to get around this branch," he said.

"No. No. I'm coming up."

A man walked up to Jimmy. "Let him die," he said. "The piece of shit deserves it."

"Shut up." said Jimmy. "He's my friend."

"He ain't nobody's friend," said the man.

"He's mine."

Jimmy belted onto the tree and began to climb.

Dallas unbelted.

"No. Don't un-belt. Cut the branch, Dallas," Jimmy shouted.

"No. Fuck it."

"Jesus Dallas. Get your belt on."

Dallas held the end of the belt in one hand. He threw it, but it flopped and didn't make it around the trunk.

"Hold it, Dallas. Just wait. Don't throw it again."

Dallas pulled the belt back, and a drop of sweat went into his eye.

"Damn." He, wiped it away.

He looked down and saw Jimmy climbing.

Dallas was exhausted, shaking, holding the tree with one hand, in fear.

"One more time," he said.

Then, Dallas's whole body gave out. He took hold of the branch with both hands, gripping it tightly. His hooks slipped out of the tree.

Dallas grunted, and his mind felt cloudy, disconnected.

"Hold on Dallas. Don't let go. I'm on my way up."

Jimmy went full speed, bark flying as he climbed.

115

"Jesus. Hold on, Dal."

Dallas tried to pull his body up, to wrap his forearm around the branch.

"Oh, God. Oh, God help. Help God…"

Dallas's hands slipped. He felt them slide as he fell.

—35

DALLAS SPENT a year back in Brazil where costs were lower and where he had a house that was paid for, so he could take his time recuperating from the fall. He would lie in bed for hours, and then, at lunchtime, crouch over, pull himself up with a cane, and meander through the apartment for exercise. Sometimes, he walked around in circles in the living room. Other times, he paced up and down the hallway.

This is when he discovered the internet. He looked up words he didn't understand, phrases, fascinating facts and people, works of art, military campaigns, anything he could think of that would occupy his mind.

He created a profile on the network Joy was using and found friends and family he hadn't seen or spoken to in years.

One of them was Maria, an eccentric cousin with a wild imagination. She was living in Romania, and she kept him up at night talking about Romanian independence and spirituality.

Then, an old face appeared, along with good memories. Don Junior, Dallas' uncle who was actually five years younger than Dallas.

"My goodness! I haven't seen that face since Grandad's funeral!" Dallas laughed. "Where are you, friend?"

Then, he saw the many posts, the long list of condolences.

"Sorry…"

"Can't believe you're gone."

"Will miss you, brother."

"Forever in my memory!"

"Why did you have to go so young?"

"Missing you."

The list went on and on.

Dallas read every one. His eyes stung with unshed tears.

How old were you, Don?

Don Junior was thirty-two.

"God almighty!" Dallas said.

The messages were dated two days before.

"Funeral services will be held in Casper, Wyoming, tomorrow."

"Oh God!" Dallas said. "I missed you by two days, brother."

He continued to go through the pictures and the statements.

Don Junior was living in abject poverty, thankful to be working as a janitor in a convenience store.

"I missed you by two days," Dallas kept saying.

Finally, he lowered his head and crossed his fingers to pray.

"Grandad, I'm sorry," he said. "But Don Junior was always a man, like you taught him, holding up his end, working, not taking handouts. We should've helped him more, just a little more, I know."

Dallas tightened his grip. His crossed fingers dug into his skin.

"He's up there with you now – where he belongs – with his best friend, his father…Sorry Grandad. Please forgive me."

—36

TREVOR PUSHED GABI through the front door of their house in a wheelchair, their eldest child Sofia walking behind. She held her newborn.

"Well Gabi, did I do good?" Trevor asked. "You have your second child."

Gabi looked up at him but couldn't speak. Here, she had just gone through childbirth, and he was taking the credit.

~   ~   ~

Shortly after the second child, Todd's birth, Gabi noticed that Trevor came home later and later, always with odd excuses. He went to the supermarket and bought something that wasn't needed, and spent hours doing it.

Of course, sex became less and less important too. The passion, the interest from her wasn't there.

Seldom did she think about it – need it – want it. She had two children now. Her thoughts were on other things, far more important.

To be honest, she thought, she'd never felt strong love for Trevor, nor he for her. Their love was always that of feasibility, necessity, something you do, because you're an adult. It was right and made sense, she thought, despite the fact that they shared no passion whatsoever. Neither one of them was guilty, but neither was innocent either. They always knew yet seldom admitted this inconvenient truth.

Yes, their marriage was doomed from the onset, and Dallas' short encounter in the beginning, regardless of how brief it was, no matter how much Gabi denied it, was an irreversible destructive force.

So, fifteen years of marriage, after many affairs, only one by Gabi, and with two children between them, she left the Catholic church and got a divorce.

—37

AFTER DALLAS RECUPERATED, he and Joy returned the US and purchased a house in Georgetown, Texas, the conservative suburb north of Austin.

He worked odd jobs – sometimes as a mechanic – sometimes installing cable TV. And on the weekends, he worked at a full-service gas station.

Dallas had numerous affairs, and he suspected Joy did the same. None of them mattered. That's not to say Dallas didn't have feelings for the women he slept with. They were just things he did – like painting a house or doing the laundry. He didn't even understand why he did it. The sex wasn't any better than what he had with Joy.

Then, like playing a game of darts with a child, winning or losing didn't matter. As a matter of fact, nothing mattered.

That's when his second son came, born on the twenty-ninth of August.

His boys grew up fast and serious. The eldest Aaron, played football for Georgetown High as a freshman, while the youngest, Donovan struggled to learn the alphabet.

The day after Donovan's sixth birthday – on a Sunday – Dallas left his job, but his truck didn't start. So, he walked the five blocks to his house.

Joy had just gotten out of the shower. Dallas took off his pants, threw them in the laundry basket, and sat on the bed.

"Don't sit there with your dirty underwear," said Joy.

"Why do you care?" Dallas asked her. "You sleep on the couch anyway. This is my bed."

"I hate the smell, your mother's smell. When I clean the sheets, and they stain so easily."

"Yeah. Yeah," Dallas stood, walked to the shower, turned-on the water, and stripped naked, as Joy did her hair behind him.

He stepped into the shower without testing the temperature. Then he adjusted it and peed.

"Are you peeing in the shower?" asked Joy.

"No."

"I can smell it." she said.

"Okay, I'm peeing. What a sense of smell. I'll never understand."

"I told you not to pee in the shower."

"Okay. I'm done."

Joy pulled two hairpins, releasing her hair, as she shook her head.

Dallas lathered up and shampooed. Then, he rinsed and turned off the water.

There was a long silence as Dallas stood in the shower, watching the drops of water fall from his nose.

Then, Joy laughed.

"What's so funny?" Dallas pulled open the curtain, grabbed a towel, and dried his face.

"Nothing. Forget it," she said.

"Okay. So, you wanna have fun?"

"Maybe…"

Dallas got out of the shower. He ran his hands through Joy's hair.

"Your hands are still wet," she said.

"So?"

"Dry them off."

"Are the kids watching TV?" he asked.

"Yes. I think so." Joy grinned again.

"What's so funny?" he asked.

Joy pulled away from Dallas and stared at him through the mirror.

"You remember that woman?"

"Which woman?"

"That woman you had an affair with."

"Which one?" he repeated.

Joy laughed. "The Brazilian one. A long time ago."

"Yes." It was all he could say.

"You know, I called her."

How would I know that? he thought.

"When?"

"When we were in Brazil," Joy said.

"Oh, okay," Dallas said, his head spinning. "You called her?"

"I told her to leave you alone," said Joy. "You know what she said?"

"No. What?"

"She began to cry and said you two were soulmates." Joy laughed. "That's what she said."

His gut contracted as if someone had kicked him. Dallas stared at Joy as she continued to curl, then pin up her hair, then let it down, and pin it up again.

"I'm sorry, Joy. What did you say?"

"I said that when I asked her to leave you alone, she said you two were, soulmates, and she wouldn't leave you alone."

Dallas glanced down, and then around the bathroom, and then out to the window. He didn't say a thing.

Joy looked at him and then back at her hair.

"Can you believe she said that?" Joy smiled.

Dallas gritted his teeth, looking out the window; the tree in the breeze, the wooden fence that he and Aaron built.

He turned to Joy. "Now, tell me the truth," he said, very calmly.

"What?" She had no idea, after years of disciplined restraint by him, how extremely dangerous this territory was.

"In the beginning, a long time ago, remember that guy, James. Remember him?"

Joy stared at herself in the mirror, as if looking into a distant place that she understood all too well.

"Yes?" she said.

"Did you cheat on me with him?"

There was a long silence.

"You did, didn't you?" Dallas said.

Joy smiled.

"Well? Tell me."

Joy didn't turn from the mirror. Then, she laughed. "Yes, I did."

Dallas stepped back. It was as if a burden – a load – an enormous weight was taken from his soul. Everything began to make sense.

Joy still didn't look in his direction. She kept her eyes on her hair, as if within her jumbled auburn curls, she could find a hiding spot.

Dallas smiled, but not a smile of kindness or love. Devious, cruel thoughts smashed in his mind. Ideas that he forged through years of miscalculations were being reworked, the sums changed.

Dallas took another step back. Then another and another, farther and farther, until he bumped into the bathroom wall.

"You did."

"Yes, I did," she said, without shame or emotion.

Dallas smirked. Tears welled up. He didn't – he couldn't – understand.

"So, why did you climb out the window and threaten to kill yourself when I wanted to go see Gabriela?"

He'd finally said her name after years of not wanting to hear or know anyone with the name. He had finally said it.

"I just didn't want you to be with her." Joy's voice was so matter of fact that he could barely understand what she was saying.

"And that's why you did it?" He shook his head.

"I'd never kill myself." Joy laughed. "You should know that."

"Damn," he said under his breath. His voice became distant, almost silent.

Dallas bit his lip, watching Joy laugh. He began to laugh too.

So, Joy laughed more.

Dallas walked across the bathroom.

"So, that's why your cousins laughed at me. They all knew you cheated on me. Your whole family knew. You went back and fucked him, right?"

All the smiles, all the laughter now made sense to him.

"Don't do anything stupid, Dallas," she said.

"You held that over my head for sixteen fucking years. Sixteen years you screamed, 'How dare you? You cheated on me.' Screaming and crying."

"Oh, stop. It wasn't that bad. Don't do anything stupid."

"Oh. You think I'm gonna do something stupid? What, like this?"

Dallas pulled the lid off the toilet and threw it into the mirror.

Bang. The mirror shattered.

"Stop." screamed Joy.

"What. Like this?"

Dallas ripped the shower curtain down.

"Is that what you're talking about?"

Joy screamed as Dallas sunk his fist into the wall – through the sheetrock – clear to the other side.

"You're insane," screamed Joy.

"Oh. I'm insane now. You have nothing to do with that, right? And me going to jail for your brother and breaking my hand. You're innocent."

Dallas picked up the laundry basket and repeatedly slammed it to the floor until it broke to pieces.

"Stop," screamed Joy. She ran out of the bathroom in just her towel. Dallas ran out too, and then realized he was naked, so he grabbed a pair of shorts and put them on. As he chased Joy, he pulled pictures off the wall, turning over tables and throwing chairs out windows.

Joy ran out of the house and across the street.

Dallas was right behind her. "Where you going?"

"I can't believe you did this," he yelled.

"Oh, stop Dallas. Don't make this a big thing."

"I manipulate you, right? You always said that." Dallas' voice was getting softer.

"You're a fucking asshole," she said.

"Then why stay married to me? Why didn't you let me get a divorce?"

"Stop…," she said. "The neighbors."

A truck pulled over, and a man got out.

Dallas turned to him. "Come on, motherfucker. You think she needs help? Come on, help her out."

"You're crazy, Dallas." Joy turned to cross the street and return to the house.

"Look at this, dude. Look." Dallas ripped Joy's towel from her body, leaving her completely naked in the street.

Joy tried to get the towel back, but Dallas threw it to the ground, stomping on it, pounding it into the dirt.

Joy screamed and ran back into the house.

"Come on, motherfucker. Defend her." Dallas walked toward the man.

The man turned, jumped back into his truck and sped away.

Pretty much what happened…

*WITH A LITTLE POETIC LICENSE.

—38

DALLAS SEARCHED THE internet for information on Gabi. He found a couple of pictures and a profile on a network.

He went through phone listings and found twenty people with the name Gabriela Rogers.

He called all of them – over and over – to see which number was hers.

Then, he remembered he had a friend, Larry Horowitz, who worked part-time as a private investigator.

To hell with it.

Dallas called his friend.

The man did a background search and found Gabriela. She was living in Clearwater, in the same field of work. He got her home and work addresses and her phone number.

"Hey, you're not gonna use it – like call this woman up and do something stupid, are you?" asked the private investigator. "I don't want to get in trouble."

"No. Of course not," said Dallas, "You know me. I'm married. Hard-working. I'd never do that. Do you know if she's married?"

"Wait. Hold on. Why do you want this woman's phone number?"

"That's simple," he said, and did some fast thinking.

"Oh?"

"Yes. I'm doing a Brazilian genealogy study, just ask a question about European heritage. We're trying to find-out the difference...the difference between Brazilian blood and Portuguese..."

"I didn't know you were into that," said the investigator.

"Yeah, I've always found that stuff interesting." said Dallas. "And did you know astrology has a great deal to do with how we name our children?" said Dallas.

"Is that right?"

"Yes. Specifically, the middle name..."

"Yeah, right. I don't know what you're planning Dallas. Don't give my name to anyone, or I'll kick your ass."

The line went dead.

Dallas dialed Gabi's number and got her voicemail.

"Gabi, this is Dallas. I know you remember me. I have to see you."

He hung up and called again.

"Gabi, it's been sixteen years, but I have to see you. I want to kiss you. Hold you. I want to make love to you, have a child with you. Call me."

—39

GABI KNELT in her garden, weeded a small area, dug down, and planted a red passiflora she'd just purchased at the nursery.

Two more to go...

The cool ocean breeze, the smell of salt water, the open sky paralleling the ocean, and her children's laughter, were the way life was supposed to be—far removed from her childhood in São Paulo with the car horns, the screams, the fights, the fear, and the hunger. Her children were growing up in paradise, in a dream—perfect, manicured—and she was the master, the one that provided everything.

"Mom, Mom."

Gabi looked at Sofia, a copy of herself, with long, flowing black hair and round Portuguese eyes.

"What, Sofia?"

"Todd hit me."

"Well, hit him back," said Gabi.

"No!" said the little girl.

Gabi sighed. "Oh well."

Just then, her cellphone rang. Gabi got up and walked over to the table, where she left it. She didn't recognize the number, a Texas number. Then, the call went to voicemail.

Gabi walked over to the spigot, turned on the water, and rinsed the dirt from her hands.

The phone rang again.

Again? Oh, my hands are wet.

"Mom," called Sofia. "The phone is ringing."

"I know, sweetheart."

Gabi wiped her hands on her pants and walked back to the table, and saw the number. It went to voicemail again.

Hmmm...The same number.

Gabi called her voicemail and listened to the first two messages, from yesterday, both from work.

Oh, I didn't know Becky called.

Then, she heard his voice.

"Oh my God."

Memories, that voice, things she hadn't thought of in years, this man, this crazy time of her life. She thought all of that was over, buried in the past, forgotten. The memories came back like waves that she wanted to avoid, but couldn't.

Gabi looked at her children.

She stepped backward, still wiping her hands on her pants, shaking her head. She closed her eyes and felt dizzy, trying to stop the spinning in her head. Just focus on the clouds in the sky, the breeze, the smell of her flowers...

"Mommy, Mommy," said Sofia.

~   ~   ~

Dallas called the number each day for a week, leaving various messages, one crazier than the next. He tried to provoke her, saying anything he could think of to get Gabi to respond.

—40

GABI COULDN'T HOLD IT in anymore. She picked up the phone and dialed.

When her sister answered, she said, "Gen, you won't believe who called me."

"Oh?"

"You won't believe it," said Gabi.

"Dallas," said Gen.

"What? How did you know?"

"I always knew," said Gen. "I just knew sooner or later he would."

"That's crazy," said Gabi.

"Gabi, that type of love you had…" Gen paused.

"What?"

"I saw it all from a distance, Gabi. Things like that don't just happen. It never happened to me. You were in the middle of the storm, so you couldn't see."

A storm. Yes, that's what it felt like. Gabi didn't know if she dared step back into it, even momentarily.

"What should I do? He keeps leaving messages."

"You haven't talked with him?"

"No. You don't remember what he did to me? I went all the way to Brazil to see him, and he never came."

"I wonder why. He loved you."

"No, he didn't," said Gabi.

"You really believe he didn't love you?"

"I think he's crazy. He left all kinds of messages."

"Like what?"

"Talking about sex and crazy things. I haven't seen him in sixteen years."

"People change," Gen said. "If he's crazy, you had better be careful. You have too much to lose. Still, I don't think it would hurt to talk to him. Aren't you curious?"

"Yes, a little," said Gabi.

"You're divorced. Just talk with him."

"Hold on. I've got another call." Then, Gabi saw the number. "Oh my God."

"What? Oh, I know," Gen said. "It's him, right?"

"Yes."

"Answer it," she said.

"No way. I'm not the same person. I'm an executive, and I eat men like him for lunch."

"You're still Gabi," Gen said.

"No. I'm not."

"You're still a woman."

"What should I do? He won't stop calling me."

"What do you think he'll do?" asked Gen.

"There's no telling. You don't know Dallas. He's wild. I mean, he's really wild," said Gabi.

"He's just like other men," Gen said.

"No. You don't know him. As a matter of fact, I never want you to know him."

"What's that supposed to mean?"

"Never mind."

"Gabi, maybe you don't know him either," Gen said. "Is he bad?"

"Yes, he is. He's terrible. I might have to kill him."

Gen laughed.

"I'm serious. I wonder how much that'd cost," she said.

"Yeah right, little Miss Mafia."

"I think he's a womanizer, Gen."

"Well, then go have fun."

"No. I don't know…"

"Maybe he's spinning a web for you, Gabi. You think about that?"

"What kind of web?" asked Gabi. "He thinks I'm still married."

Gen sighed. "Maybe you should do the safe thing and just tell him to leave you alone. If that's what you want."

After they hung up, she called voicemail, her fingers shaking. Her heart pounded as she listened to another crazy message.

~   ~   ~

Then, two days later, on February 12, Gabi made up her mind.

It was exactly 12:46 AM when she called Dallas.

She remembered Dallas turned off his phone at night because he had difficulty sleeping.

Sure enough, his phone was off and she left the following message.

"Dallas, do not reach out to me again. Do not try to see me. I do not welcome your efforts. My life has changed tremendously in the last fifteen years, and I am happy, really happy. What happened between us is in the past, and it has no place and no chance in this present time. You will not hear from me again. Wish you all the best. Goodbye."

For Gabi, rejection was too painful, the fear too great. Love is submission, exposing ourselves, our weaknesses, naked, all our ugliness, rough edges, pain. While she had been focused on her children, her family, those dependent on her, she gave up on herself.

Sometimes, we find someone who will embrace us entirely. They bring forth our souls, without shame. Fear becomes a smile. Pain is laughter. All our humanity is beautiful. The rough edges of our souls, forged over years of hardship, fit together like pieces in a puzzle.

Gabi didn't need to fear Dallas, but she did. She told herself Dallas and his advances were too childish to the older, wiser, stable mother she had become.

—41

A DAY BEFORE GABI'S birthday she received an overnight package at work, a large envelope. This was odd. It seldom happened. The envelope was from Georgetown, Texas.

She looked at the sender's name.

"Dallas," she yelled. "That asshole. Now, he's sending packages at work."

Gabi called Ship Express and asked for the manager.

"This is Gabriela Rogers," she said. "I received an unwanted package from someone who is harassing me. I will not accept it and do not want any more packages from this person."

"He's harassing you?" the manager asked.

"Yes. I told him not to contact me."

"Okay. We will be over to pick-up the package, and I'll contact the sender personally. What's the tracking number?"

Gabi gave her the number, and the woman reassured her that she would call Dallas immediately.

Dallas, saw the number on his phone.

Is it Gabi? She must have gotten the package.

But when he answered the phone, it wasn't Gabi's voice he heard.

"Hi. This is Ship Express. Is this Dallas?"

"Yes."

"Did you send a package to a woman in Clearwater, Florida?"

"Yes," said Dallas. "Why?"

"The package was denied by the receiver, and I've been advised to contact you. We will not accept shipments from you. Do not attempt to send another package with us."

"Whatever," said Dallas.

"Do you want me to send the package back to you?"

"No," he said. "Keep it. Throw it away. I don't care."

"Do you give me permission to open the package – to further investigate?" she asked.

"Yeah, yeah, yeah. Throw me in jail lady, if you find something bad. How's that?"

"Okay, sir. I don't think you're taking this seriously."

"No. That's not it," said Dallas. "I simply don't give a shit, lady."

An hour later, Christine got the envelope back from Gabi. She held it in her hands, and Dallas gave her verbal permission that was recorded, so she could now open it.

Christine took a boxcutter and slit the envelope open. There was a letter, and a white box with one red rose inside.

She opened the letter and read…

"Oh my God." she gasped.

Christine called Gabi.

"Hello?" said Gabi.

"Mrs. Rogers?" asked Christine.

"Yes."

"This is Christine, from Ship Express…"

"Yes?"

"I have a question for you…" said Christine.

"Oh?"

"This is a personal question. I'd never ask you this if you didn't contact me…" said Christine.

Gabriela was unsure, worried… "What is it?" she said.

"Did you have an affair with this man at some point?"

"Don't ask me that!" said Gabi.

Christine was silent…

"I don't think that question is appropriate." demanded Gabi.

There was a long wait…

"What do you want me to do with this package?" asked Christine.

"I don't care. I don't want anything to do with this. I'm contacting the authorities about this man."

"Then, maybe you want to read what he wrote," said Christine.

"No, I don't." said Gabi.

"I think you should, if you're gonna call the police."

Gabi thought…

"What's that supposed to mean? What did he say?"

"Mrs. Rogers, you need to read this for yourself. I won't read it over the phone."

"Oh no." Gabi sighed.

Gabi's fingers tapped her desk, in deep thought.

"Okay, I'll be there in a few minutes…"

Gabi hung-up, banged her desk with her fist, and told her secretary she was leaving, and would be back shortly.

Ten minutes later, Gabi arrived at Ship Express' office.

"Mrs. Rogers, here's the envelope." Christine handed it to her…

Gabi opened the letter and read…

Gabi,

I didn't know how to tell you this, I didn't want to say it over voicemail. I never told you why I did what I did.

I held it in for years, trying to do the right thing.

My wife told me what you told her, when she called you, and told you to leave me alone – that you thought we were soulmates.

And remember when we were supposed to meet in São Paulo?

The reason I didn't go, was because my wife climbed out on the ledge of our apartment and threatened to leap-off and commit suicide, with our two-year-old son in the other room.

"Oh, my God." Gabi looked at Christine. Christine tapped her fingers on the counter.

Chills ran up Gabi's spine.

Gabi didn't want to read-on, but she did…

I wanted to tell you, but I couldn't. I wanted to say, I love you. I'm sorry I didn't make it to São Paulo, it was the biggest mistake of my life. Sorry. Sorry.

Now, my wife admitted, she cheated on me, before we cheated on our spouses.

I have to see you. I love you.

There's so much to say – that I have to explain...You must understand something.

Can we talk?

Gabi covered her mouth...

"Okay, Mrs. Rogers, how am I supposed to deal with this?"

"I don't know..." said Gabi.

Gabi handed the letter back to Christine.

Christine took it, folded it, and placed it back in the envelope.

Gabi turned and left.

—42

DALLAS LISTENED to Gabi's message over and over.

"In this present time…" he repeated.

Am I supposed to get a divorce?

"I'm happy, really happy…"

He did a search on the phrase and found a Christian song for children…

Is she telling me she has two children? If so, why speak in codes?

Does she know I'm still married?

Dallas called Gabi and left another message…

"Are you speaking in codes? Why can't we just talk? I have so much to tell you. Call me Gabi."

Then Dallas called again and left another message.

"Gabi, what are you trying to tell me? Is something wrong. What the hell is this? I hate to speak to your voicemail. Call me."

A couple days later, Dallas gave up.

He called and left the following message:

"You know what you are – a woman who's lost. You talk in riddles – too arrogant to speak to me. You're the type of woman who hates real men. You end up hating yourself and confused."

Dallas threw his phone to the ground.

He went to pick it up.

"Bitch." he yelled.

He jumped up and down on the phone, smashing it into pieces.

Dallas, picked-up the phone and threw it in the trash.

—43

DALLAS GOT A JOB at the local cable office, cutting trees away from the cable system.

Seldom – if ever – did he work nights, but there were always exceptions.

A crew needed help. So, Dallas got in his truck and drove-out. He met the crew.

A cable was cut. Customers were out of service and the crew's lasher was stuck in a branch.

The cable crew still needed to hang ten more spans through overgrown cedars and oaks.

Of course, the city of Austin, having been taken-over by hardcore environmentalists years ago, demanded permits if someone, so much as touched an oak tree.

Dallas was the only one ornery enough, not to care.

"You know they'll charge you $20,000 dollars if you cut a root. Branches must be in the millions," said a stout guy in a cowboy hat.

Dallas smiled. "Yes, sir."

He cranked-up his chainsaw.

"They sue us if their service doesn't work, and sue us if we fix it. Idiots – all of them. Let them sue me. I live in an RV," Dallas said, with his chainsaw blaring.

The men around Dallas laughed as he cut into the trees without safety equipment or a hardhat.

Dallas had all the limbs dropped before sunrise.

He was pulling the branches to the front yard of a house – throwing them in piles – when a man approached.

Dallas was the only worker onsite. The others had left the area, hours ago.

"What do you think you're doing?" asked the man.

Dallas stared. He was used to dealing with angry homeowners.

"Hello, sir."

"The hell you think you're doing?" the man asked again.

"Working on the outage," said Dallas.

The homeowner called the phone number on the side of Dallas' truck.

"Hello. I'm calling to complain, about an idiot at my house."

"Well, you talk with them," said Dallas with a smile, and walked away.

"Where do you think you're going?" the man demanded.

"You're talking with my bosses. You don't need to talk with me anymore," said Dallas.

The man followed him. "Son, you stand right there."

"I'll stand where the fuck I want."

The homeowner pulled the phone from his ear. "What did you say?"

"You heard me," Dallas said. "Don't tell me what to do."

"You know what you did?" the man demanded. "Well, come over here. Look." The man walked to the corner of his next-door neighbor's yard and pointed to a large rut in the grass.

Dallas walked over, all the while staring at the ground.

"You did that, dumbass."

Still staring at the ground, Dallas turned to the man. "I didn't do that, you fucking dipshit."

The homeowner dropped the phone, stepped back, and swung, hitting Dallas flush on his left temple.

Dallas' head went back, but not far. Dallas didn't look away.

The man's eyes grew large. "Oh shit." he said.

Dallas reached-up – took hold of the man's head – snaked his right arm over his neck and his left under – pulled him down – tightened his grip – then raked his fingernails across the man's face, over and over again.

Dallas didn't know what he was doing – he just did it.

He brought the man down to the ground – tightening his grip every second – continuing to rake his fingers into the man's eyes – across the man's face.

The man gasped for air. His arms flailed at Dallas' side. He was running-out of air – coughing – choking.

Dallas realized the man was losing his breath. So, he let him go.

Both men stood.

The homeowner's face was gushing blood from various cuts.

"Oh no." said Dallas, looking at the flesh under his fingernails.

"I'm calling the police." said the man.

The home owner thought – shook his head – remembering he swung first.

"No. I'm not going to call the police."

"Good idea," said Dallas.

The man kept walking backward and took a seat in his truck.

"Look, sir," said Dallas. "I didn't make this rut, but I did chop the branches down in your backyard, but I'm done. And if you aren't going to call the police. I'm leaving."

"Stop," he said.

Dallas turned.

"What?"

"Sir?" said the man.

"Yes?" said Dallas.

"You need to go to church, sir," the man said.

Dallas stood there, frowning.

"You need to go to church with me," the man's eyes filled with tears. "I want to take you to church."

Dallas looked puzzled.

"Will you let me take you to church?" said the homeowner.

Dallas breathed heavy. The man approached Dallas, and put his hand-out. Dallas' eyes filled with tears…

Dallas reached-out. The two men shook hands.

"I'll go to church with you Sir," said Dallas.

"My name is Greg by the way," blood was still pouring out of the man's face.

"My name is Dallas."

"Nice to meet you Dallas."

"Nice to meet you too, Greg."

—44

DALLAS WENT TO CHURCH every Sunday. He even went to counseling for his marriage, and talked with his cousin, Maria in Romania about the responsibilities of a husband. He even saw a psychiatrist – but there was no use.

He told everyone he was getting a divorce no matter what.

Then, he began talking about going to Gabi.

Everyone begged him not to go. Surely, he would end up in jail.

Dallas was puzzled, with tunnel vision. He couldn't get Gabi out of his mind, what he had done, and how he had hurt her. He couldn't forgive himself. He had to talk with her – some way.

Then, three months after he stopped calling Gabi, he dialed her number

"Please leave a message…"

"Gabi. I love you. Please talk with me. Everything I've done is for you. I've been lost without you. I've gone to jail twice. If I go back, I'm afraid I'll die. I don't know what to tell you. I love you. I'm sorry. God, I'm sorry I didn't make it to São Paulo."

He hung up the phone, then called back.

"Gabi, I have $10,000 saved. I'll give it all to you if you just let me look in your eyes."

Five minutes later, he received a text message on his phone.

"This is harassment now. Leave me alone. I don't want your money. If you persist, I'll contact the police."

Dallas called back immediately. The phone went to voicemail.

"Call the fucking police! Press your goddamn charges, Gabi. I'll plead guilty to everything! I swear to God I will. I don't care. I'm guilty of them all, anyway."

When Dallas hung up the phone, he crossed his finger and prayed.

"Jesus, forgive me. I'm sorry. I know she's married. I don't understand what's going on. I just want to see her. I don't think that's a sin. I'm sorry."

—45

"COME ON, lift that up. Give it all you got, son." said Dallas.

"I am," said Aaron.

"No, you're not. Lift. You got strength. Use it."

"This is all I got, Dad."

"Lift. Now."

"Stop this." The boy seemed ready to cry. He dropped the two-by-six, and stared at Dallas.

"Get your ass over here, Aaron."

"You don't have to use bad language."

"There are times when bad language is needed, just like violence, and at this moment, I'm gonna use bad language. Now, get your ass back here, right now."

Aaron glared at him.

"Get over here. Lift it up."

Aaron walked back and grabbed the board.

"There you go – get low – bend your legs – put your body under it," said Dallas.

"Show me," said Aaron.

"No. You do it."

"Why can't you just show me?"

"Do it."

The teenager got low, and lifted the board in the air…

"Now, hold it there for as long as you can. Let's see if I can get the screws in," said Dallas.

"I can't hold it much longer."

"Yes, you can. Just hold it a little longer, just a little longer."

Aaron's arms began to tremble.

"It's too heavy. It's slipping."

"Just hold it there." Dallas slowly placed a screw in his fingers and began drilling.

"Stop shaking, or we'll have to do it over," he told Aaron.

"I can't hold it anymore. My arms."

"That's why you need to get stronger. Hold it, son. Let me get one more in. Good. And now you can let go."

Dallas got down from the ladder and stepped backward. "There it is," he said.

Aaron's arms came down. He rubbed them over and over.

"Look at that. Come here," said Dallas.

Aaron was still red-faced.

"Come here, son. Look."

Aaron stood beside his father.

Dallas put his arm around the boy.

Aaron shrugged him off.

"Stop that crap kid. I'll kick your ass right here."

"You think you can?" Aaron asked.

"I know I can. Now, shut up, and look at what we did. And you held it all up," said Dallas.

Aaron looked up, at the cover of the barbecue pit.

"Look at that. How does it look?"

Aaron smiled. "That looks good."

Dallas put his arm around his son's shoulders again. This time, the boy let him. "You did good," said Dallas.

"Thanks, Dad."

"Listen, what's going on between your mom and me, it's not easy. I know. But, that's life. Don't let it get between us, okay?"

Aaron stared at his father. He didn't say a word.

"The divorce was finalized last week. You know that, right?"

Aaron nodded.

"Yeah, your mom told you?"

"Yes."

"Come here."

Aaron let his father embrace him.

Dallas took hold of his son's face.

"Look at me," he said.

Their eyes met.

"That doesn't mean I stop being your father, right?"

Aaron nodded.

"You know I love you."

"Yes."

"Always, and forever," Dallas said.

—46

DALLAS WAS DRIVING to work when his radio lost reception. He spun the knob, searching for a station. The radio tuned-in…

The song was Tracy Chapman's, *Baby Can I Hold You.*

The melody was slow…Tracy began to sing; all that can be said is sorry…

"Sorry," said Dallas.

Tracy sang about forgiveness…and the years that have gone by…

"Forgive me," said Dallas.

Everything came back, Gabi's eyes, her smile, her skin, that smile that melted his soul.

Tracy sang on and Dallas sang along.

"Forgive me."

I have to look in her eyes and tell her I'm sorry…She has to know. I have to see her.

Dallas came to a stoplight in the left-hand turn lane.

He looked around and then behind him.

The arrow turned green for him to turn left. A car behind him honked.

Dallas turned right across all the lanes, through the intersection, in front of everyone.

He drove to a gas station, fueled up, and called his ex-wife.

"Dallas?" Joy answered the phone.

"Hi, Joy."

"Yes?"

"You have to know, Joy. I'm going to go see Gabi."

"Where are you? What are you doing, Dallas?"

"I don't know. I'm just going to do it," he said.

"With the money we have saved?" Her voice rose.

"Yes."

"Don't do it, Dallas. Don't do anything crazy. This divorce is temporary. We both know that."

"I'm just letting you know. Tell the kids I won't see them this weekend. Okay?"

Dallas hung up. *Okay*, he thought. *Where's a map?*

—47

AS **DALLAS** *DROVE* to Clearwater, along I-10, across bridges, over the marshland of Louisiana, staring out, dreaming, it all became clear. That is, why Gabi left such a trivial message.

Gabi is still married. She's getting a divorce, and she's afraid of her husband.

"Oh my God. Of course," Dallas announced as he almost lost control of his truck.

Dallas remembered Gabi saying that her husband went through her things and found out all kinds of stuff. He kept track of her.

What if I hurt Gabi with all my phone calls – she wanted me to leave her alone, like she said, "In this present time"? That's why she left the coded message...She couldn't just come out and say she had two children. Her husband was watching her. Oh, my God. How stupid am I?

I might have ruined her chance to have custody of the children. He's going to use my phone calls in court, against Gabi!

It's all my fault.

What can I do to help?

Dallas pulled his truck over, got out his phone, and called Gabi.

He had to leave a coded message himself. He knew she'd understand.

What reference should I use? Phantom of the Opera. No time to figure out everything now. I'll do it later.

155

I have to make her husband think I gave up, because Gabi was completely faithful.

If Gabi's husband tries to use my voicemails against her in a court, this one will prove she did everything right. She kept me away and refused me.

The call went directly to voicemail. "Please leave a message…"

"Gabi. I give up. You refuse to see me. I can't stand it anymore. You're so cruel and mean. I hate you. Oh, how I hate you. I just wanted to see you, asshole. I guess your place is in an office."

Dallas hung up and screamed, "Damn. I'm such a fucking idiot."

But that has to be the reason. Why else would she not talk with me? And that's why she couldn't meet me. "

It all made sense to Dallas. But it didn't stop him from going to Clearwater. It just changed his approach.

He spent the rest of the drive thinking of ways he could see her, without her husband finding out.

He came up with a good one. *Last of the Mohicans, Phantom of the Opera,* and *Dr. Zhivago.*

But how will I help her get the divorce and custody of the children?

That was far more difficult and demanded a great deal more thought.

—48

AFTER TWO DAYS walking the streets through downtown Clearwater and along the coast, around sand dunes, trying to figure out a way to help Gabi get full custody, Dallas took a seat on a dirty bench. He sifted sand between his toes.

Okay, it'll be tough, but I have to do it.

I'll hire a prostitute to seduce her husband, get pictures to present at the trial...

That'll get her custody and fix the mess I made.

I'll contact her sister, Gen. She can get the pictures to Gabi without her husband knowing. This will work. I know it.

I need to find a good-looking woman, but not too good-looking. He'll get suspicious. Maybe someone he knows. I have to find out where he works.

I wonder if there's a way to find that girl he cheated on Gabi with the first time?

If I could only contact Gabi...But, she had to send that coded message. He must be practically holding her captive. That son of a bitch. I'm going to get him good. If I saw him now, I'd beat the shit out him...Fucking with Gabi like that.

Dallas called his detective friend again.

"Hey, I need a woman to seduce someone. Do you do that kind of stuff?"

"What are you talking about?" he demanded.

"Price is not a problem. I got a lot of money saved up. I need to seduce a guy and get pictures to present in court. Like I said, price isn't a problem."

"Ah, man. What are you talking about? Where are you?"

"Florida," said Dallas. No point in lying.

"Does this have anything to do with that phone number I gave you?"

"Forget about that."

"Dallas," he said. "Swear to God, if someone contacts me, I don't know who you are. I think you have the wrong number. Bye."

The line went dead.

—49

DALLAS WAS IN a self-imposed prison, made of his wife's lies. Like a tiger pacing back and forth in a cage. Planning. Drooling. Hungry. Staring. Stupid. Frustration building day by day, hour by hour, for sixteen years.

To Dallas, when the bars of his cell were broken and his mind and heart were free to roam without guilt, nothing mattered! No law. No reason. No decency. The tiger ran, experiencing and testing his newfound freedom. Whether or not Gabriela was still married or divorced – even if she was deeply in love with her husband, or another man for that matter – made no difference to Dallas. What drove him wasn't right or wrong. It was animal.

After years of life making sense, adult thoughts, responsibilities, right, wrong, budgets, nodding and smiling at lies, slowly losing his hunger. Yes. Yes. Yes…

No! The charade was over! The game was up.

Dallas now, spent his thoughts justifying his most base instinct. He was going to see Gabriela, no matter what!

Still believing Gabi was married, Dallas went to the Marquee Theater on Ohio Street and spoke to the manager, negotiating with him to show his triple feature, *The Last of the Mohicans, Phantom of the Opera*, and then *Dr. Zhivago*.

The theater manager was confused at first, so Dallas changed gears and asked for a "Private showing," of the three movies, just for him and a woman who might be joining him. That made more sense to the manager.

"A private showing," he said.

Because the theater was owned entirely by a family, not a chain, and they had a digital projector that could be connected to a DVD player, money was the only obstacle. Dallas set the showing for an off-day for the theater; a Wednesday, beginning at 4 PM and playing until finished, about eleven o'clock that night.

"How much do you want?" he asked the manager.

The manager was a short man in his thirties, constantly biting his lower lip. That's why Dallas thought he had a chance. The man was nervous. Maybe he needed the money.

"Well, we usually make four to five hundred on a decent night, and I'll have to turn some people away, our regular customers."

"I see," said Dallas.

"And this isn't something I really recommend…"

Dallas cut him off. "A thousand dollars, cash!"

"You bring the DVDs?" asked the manager.

"Yes."

"A thousand dollars?"

"That's what I said."

"Done!" he said, but Dallas could tell that now he was money ahead and thinking bigger. "But what if some people want to go to the showing, my usual customers?" he asked.

"I don't care." Dallas shrugged, thinking only of Gabi. "Let them in."

~   ~   ~

He called back Larry, his detective friend and got Gabi's email.

"You know, Dallas, I looked into this woman's background," he said. "There are two court files on her."

"So?"

160

"I don't know what's in them, but I can get them for you, for a price."

"Yeah, get them," said Dallas. "How about the prostitute?"

"A prostitute, to do that will cost a lot. You can't just get one off the street, you know, but I think I found her. You might need to interview her, if you know what I mean." He laughed.

"Yeah. Okay."

Dallas thought, if he could get Gabi away from her husband, where they were together, he could explain his elaborate plan, maybe even work out the details – and a movie theater seemed like the most logical solution.

She could justify wanting to see a movie by herself, and her husband wouldn't suspect a thing.

So, Dallas began sending Gabi emails from a fictitious email account. The name of the account was Sin2HeavenPromotions@....com

The emails were disguised like promotional emails from the Marquee Theater.

The first email:

Subject: *Your place is in the ARTS, not an office!*

Coming attractions at Marquee Theater, to be shown after the storm has passed...

Two video clips from the movie *Phantom of the Opera* were attached to the email.

The first was the song "Masquerade."

Gabi received the email and couldn't help it. Her curiosity got the better of her. She had to download the file and watch.

Men and women, all wearing masquerade masks danced and sang about a masquerade ball.

The song was carefully chosen by Dallas, so Gabi knew the earlier voice message, when he called her an "asshole" was just that, a masquerade.

Gabi listened to the song and wondered.

Then, the next video, *Phantom of the Opera*'s "Why So Silent."

A heavy beat as the Phantom played by Gerard Butler walked down a staircase. Then, silence.

Gerard Butler sang about his return and his new opera, *Don Juan Triumphant.*

Gabi fell over in her chair as she heard it, laughing. Then, she pictured Dallas as Don Juan, and thought, *He must be deranged. He's gone completely insane.*

The Phantom, Gerard Butler sang on, demanding managers stay out of the arts; their place was in an office.

Gabi shook her head, smiling. Music slowed, and then the Phantom addressed Miss Christine Daaé.

There was just Gerard Butler's voice.

Gabi shook her head.

The music slowed to nothing.

The Phantom shouted that the girl belonged to him.

Oh my gosh. He has gone crazy.

Gabi wondered what Dallas was trying to say. First, the mean voicemail, and now these videos.

The confusion only worsened the situation.

The next email came.

Subject: *Coming attractions, Last of the Mohicans.*

Must see, love endures through great turmoil. Last of the Mohicans, coming to Marquee Theater as soon as possible.

Gabi watched the video attached.

Madeleine Stowe screamed; Daniel Day-Lewis had done all he could. He must leave. A raging waterfall pounded the rocks behind them.

Daniel held Madeleine Stowe in his arms and assured her, "Just stay alive, no matter what!" She has to submit to her capturers and just survive. No matter what happens he would find her.

Then Daniel leapt from the rocks, through the waterfall, down an enormous crevasse.

The videos were Dallas' signal, for Gabi to play along with his scheme, even if she didn't know what he was planning.

He thought Gabi would understand that he was preparing something. He was going to make his move.

But the results were different than his intentions. Gabi only laughed, convinced he was completely insane.

The next day, another email, and another video, again from *Phantom of the Opera*, the song "Notes."

Raoul, sang about being blind, and yet, the answer to their problem was staring them in the face – referencing Gabi's husband, Trevor – a way to ensnare their clever friend.

Dallas hoped Gabi understood that he'd figured out a way to get rid of Trevor.

The two characters, André and Firmin assured Raoul that they were listening.

So, Raoul continued with his plan—how they should play along with the Phantom's game (Trevor) and perform his work. And when Miss Daaé sings, the Phantom will attend the opera, and the doors will be barred – and Gabi and Dallas would rid themselves of Trevor!

Firmin noted that the police will be there. And Raoul exclaimed that the police will be armed.

Everyone said that the curtains will fall, and his reign will end!

Dallas hoped Gabi understood this message as it was intended. If she didn't understand everything, such as arranging the prostitute to seduce her husband, surely she'd know Dallas was arranging something to ensnare him and help end her marriage…

The following day, another email.

Subject: *Dr. Zhivago, coming to Marquee Theater.*

A passion that destroyed a nation. Love that could never be. A lifetime waiting. How could it be, but no matter, it is...

Must see. Dr. Zhivago. Coming to Marquee Theater.

The *Dr. Zhivago* video was the theatrical trailer:

Repetitive piano keys, beat…

Alec Guinness in a serious, yet quiet voice, said "I'm looking for someone."

Then a military commander was looking at Omar Sharif. He demands Sharif work as a doctor!

The scene cut to Sharif as he looked up to Julie Christie and asked if she's a nurse.

Julie Christie said "Yes," and Sharif asked her for help.

Then Christie was sitting in a wagon, looking to Sharif.

And the piano beat on...

Then Geraldine Chaplin was dancing with Omar Sharif, and she tells him that she's seen an extraordinary girl.

Then a gunshot!

Cut to Sharif addressing Rod Steiger about what happens to a girl like Christie when Steiger is done with her.

Steiger replied, "I'll give her to you."

Cut to Omar and Christie holding each other, but she's crying.

Christie screamed "Zhivago!"

Powerful music.

Sharif was holding Christie.

There's an explosion*!*

Christie stared at Sharif and asked him if he wished they met before they did – in a different time, a perfect world...

Sharif assured her that they'll go mad thinking like that.

Christie told him that she'll always think like that.

The piano slowly died away.

And that was it! Gabi had enough. She couldn't take the emotions, the sheer insanity. She didn't understand anything Dallas was trying to tell her, in his own cryptic, twisted emails, nor did she want to understand.

She deleted her email account, hoping to never hear from Dallas ever again.

~   ~   ~

Then, the day came, when all three movies played at the Marquee Theater.

Dallas' dream of seeing Gabi sitting beside him, holding his hand, slipped away like grains of sand through his fingers.

He waited, tapped his feet, watched teenagers make out through the entire triple feature.

Gabi never showed.

—50

A WOMAN WEARING a tight skirt, with very large breasts approached Trevor as he sat on a park bench eating his lunch.

"Hello," she said. "Mind if I sit beside you?"

Trevor looked up at the woman – his eyes widened at the scantily clad attire.

"Um, how was your day?" smiled the woman, wiping lipstick from her mouth.

Trevor glanced back and forth, unsure…

"My day has been fine, thanks."

The woman brushed her hair back, stared at the missing wedding ring from his finger.

"Hmm…" she thought about asking him if he was married, but thought better of it, knowing if she was to seduce him, the subject was taboo.

A bird flew over their heads and she turned abruptly brushing her breasts against his shoulder, causing him to spill his soda.

"Oops! Look what I did," she bent over, again rubbing her breasts against him, this time his thigh.

Trevor stood up, lifted his hands and just stared at the woman beneath him, as she continued to wipe his pants, lick her lips – then slowly turn upward, smiling, looking into his eyes – still on her knees…

She stopped smiling, her mouth, expression got serious – looking at the man above her.

~   ~   ~

An hour later, they were in a hotel room – having sex…

"Wait, oh wait a second," said the woman. "I need to do something," she rolled out from under Trevor.

He was in a daze, gasping for air, unsure what was happening.

"Wait? Umm…What?" he kept saying.

The woman got up, walked to the dresser, pulled out her cellphone, lifted it up to her ear as if answering a call, but secretly turned on the camera…

"Trevor, is that your name?"

"What? Umm…Yeah, my name is Trevor," he said. "Why? What are you doing? Who are you talking to?" he asked standing up, walking toward her.

"I'm programming you into my phone," she said.

"Oh, well come back to bed."

~   ~   ~

"I got the pictures in the mail!" said Dallas to his private eye friend.

"Did you notice, in the picture?" the man laughed.

"Is that really him?"

"Hey, that's him!"

"He's got a small one, doesn't he?" said the detective.

Dallas almost fell over laughing! "He's got a small little peter!"

The laughter slowly died away, and Dallas tapped his fingers.

"Hey, umm…Looks like he isn't wearing a wedding band. Is that right?"

"Yeah, I noticed that too," you want me to look in on it?"

"What?" Dallas got angry. "You mean to tell me you didn't check to see if Gabi and him were still married? You're a detective!"

"Well, we're not certain."

"Oh, come on! Did I just pay for this guy to get laid? Do they even live together?"

"They might not live in the same house," said the detective.

"Oh man! You're telling me you didn't check if they were married after you found out they lived in different houses and he wasn't wearing a wedding band?"

"Well, you said 'money's not a problem,' so I thought it really didn't matter. Now we have the pictures you wanted Dallas, and…"

Dallas hung up the phone. "Ah man, this is ridiculous!"

He took a seat – in deep thought, "So, is he married or not?"

—51

DALLAS' SAVINGS were running low when he received the package from his private-eye friend.

Finally!

Dallas held the envelope in his hands, dreaming, wondering, in fear of opening it.

What should I do?

Maybe, I should just throw it away, and go back to Texas…

Just then, he received a phone call.

He looked at his phone. It was Maria, his cousin from Romania.

"Oh, thank God you answered," said Maria.

Dallas explained where he was and what he was doing.

Maria encouraged him. "Do it, Dallas. Go and see her. You are with angels that will protect you."

"Are you sure?" asked Dallas.

"Go, find her," she insisted. "She won't reject you. Soon, you will be making love to her."

She continued to convince him of what he was afraid to believe, and when they hung up, he thought, *Well, that's it. I'm all in.*

Dallas opened the package, searching…

The first document was a marriage certificate. He threw it away.

The second was a divorce decree, finalized years ago.

Dallas sifted through the pages, dumbfounded, unsure what to think.

Gabi's been divorced the entire time?

Then, why didn't she want to talk with me?

My God!

Dallas was heartbroken. In one instant, he realized he could see her, and the next, he knew he'd go to jail.

Gabi truly had no other reason to push Dallas away other than the fact that she wanted nothing to do with him.

This can't be true.

But it was, and the more time went by, the deeper the realization sunk into his soul.

Dallas paced back and forth in his hotel room.

"Fuck it. I'm going there tomorrow," he declared.

Let's get this over with. She'll finally know I wasn't playing a game. There will be no doubt.

This isn't a matter of if. It's a matter of when, and I may never have this chance again.

Dallas called Gabi and left the following message, "Gabi, I have to prove to you that your ex was wrong. I was not a womanizer. I don't think you can throw me jail. You have too much heart. I want to put everything in your hands, everything, my entire life and future. You have to know without a doubt. There can't be any question in your mind that what I did was a mistake. I love you Gabi. I'm going to go to your work tomorrow. I have to do this. Maybe then you'll believe me."

—52

DALLAS LAY IN BED watching the clock tick, unable to stop thinking about Gabi.

It's been sixteen years since I saw her...

I'll see her tomorrow.

Dallas crossed his fingers and prayed...

"Please Jesus, I don't want to go to jail, but if I must, I will. She has to know I always loved her. I have to make this right. Please help. All I want to do is see her. If she tells me to leave, I'll leave. Swear to God I will...Jesus, help me. I don't think this is a sin. I'm divorced, and she is too."

After the prayer, he fell into a deep slumber.

He awoke at five o'clock, after only two hours of sleep. Then, he called Gabi. "Gabi, I'm going to your work. I'll be there waiting for you. I'm pretty sure you're going to call the police, but I only ask one thing, that you look me in the eyes before I go to jail. If you do that, I'll not say a word. I'll just leave. But I have to look in your eyes. That's all. I just want to do what I should've done sixteen years ago."

Dallas dressed in a gray T-shirt, worn blue jeans, his black cowboy boots, and a red baseball cap.

He drove to her office, got there at five-thirty, turned on the radio, and waited.

Phil Collins "Against All Odds" played.

Dallas wondered if the song was an omen, a good sign or a bad one. He closed his eyes, tightly, and took deep breaths.

Phil Collins sang.

After Gabi heard Dallas' voicemail, she couldn't do her hair, couldn't put on her makeup. She called everyone who worked at her office, telling them not to approach the man in the parking lot.

"Don't look at him. Don't get near him. Don't speak to him. Just go directly inside the building. I'll deal with him."

Her hands trembled. She was lost, doing everything she could to hold her life together, act like nothing affected her. She was the manager, in control of the situation.

"This man is insane," she shouted at her secretary over the phone.

"You don't have to be so loud," said Teresa the secretary.

"Oh, God. I just can't believe it. Is he still there?"

"Yes. He's sitting in his truck."

"I have to call the police," she said.

"Is this the same man who sent you the package?"

"Yes," said Gabi.

"Why don't you just talk with him?" she asked.

"He's completely insane...and dangerous," Gabi said. "He's been to jail several times, in different countries. He's crazy. What am I going to do?"

"I don't know, Gabi." Her secretary giggled.

"This isn't funny."

"I guess, call the police Gabi."

"Okay," she said. "I'm calling them."

Did you read the fine print?

—53

"PLEASE HAVE A SEAT. So, how may we help you?" said Mr. Ruiz. He was an older lawyer in a gray suit.

Gabi took a seat at a large table.

"He's called me nonstop, leaving messages, won't leave me alone. He wants to have sex. There's no telling what he'll do."

Mrs. Thoreau Esquire took a seat at the table, "Okay, who's this perv?"

"Dallas," said Gabi.

"Is that his name?" asked Mrs. Thoreau.

"No. But that's what everyone calls him," she said.

"What's his actual name?"

"I don't know."

"He uses an alias," the woman said. "Typical criminal behavior."

"No, he's not a criminal," said Gabi.

The lawyer looked puzzled. "What is he to you? How does he know you?"

"I don't want to get into that, she said. "He's bothering me. I'm a mother. He can't contact me."

"Yes, but we have to have information," Mrs. Thoreau said.

"If we take him to court, he'll defend himself. Do I have to remind you of that?" said Mr. Ruiz.

"We were friends once," said Gabi.

"Friends?" asked Mr. Ruiz.

"Okay, we were lovers."

"For how long?" asked Mrs. Thoreau.

"Twice," said Gabi.

"How long did you date him?" asked Mr. Ruiz.

"Two times," said Gabi.

"You saw him twice? Or…How should I say this without sounding intrusive…had relations?" said Mr. Ruiz.

Mrs. Thoreau frowned.

"Both," said Gabi.

"Two dates," said Mr. Ruiz.

Mrs. Thoreau's fingers tapped the table, "This doesn't matter. What was the extent of the relationship? Were you married at the time?"

"Does that matter?" Gabi wished she'd never started this conversation.

"Was he married?" asked Mr. Ruiz.

"Yes," said Gabi.

Mr. Ruiz scratched his chin.

"We met twice and then never again," she said.

"Okay. But what happened between you two?" asked Mrs. Thoreau cautiously.

"We met." Gabi took a deep breath. "We tried to divorce our spouses and marry each other."

The lawyers looked at each other.

"You mean you saw him twice…and from that, you tried to divorce your husband and marry him, and he did the same?" asked Mrs. Thoreau.

Gabi ran her hands through her hair.

Mr. Ruiz shook his head, "Sounds like a…"

"Don't say it," said Mrs. Thoreau.

"…must have been some kind of an affair," said Mr. Ruiz.

Gabi and Mrs. Thoreau's eyes met.

"Sorry. I can only imagine," said Mrs. Thoreau.

"This is going to be a tough case," said Mr. Ruiz.

"I'm going to take care of this for you," said Mrs. Thoreau. "I understand. This perv needs to be dealt with."

"Yes. But what can we do?" Gabi asked.

"We can get a restraining order. Throw him in jail."

"He'll have his day in court," said Mr. Ruiz.

"Will he be there?" asked Gabi. "I mean, will he be in court?"

"Oh, yeah. The perv will argue his case," said Mr. Ruiz.

"Please don't call him a perv," said Gabi.

The lawyers looked at each other.

Gabi continued, "I don't want to see him. He said so many things…about sex. I have a career. What a mistake he was."

"Could he say things to hurt you?" asked Mrs. Thoreau.

"Does he still love you?" said Mr. Ruiz.

"Yes. Yes." She answered them both.

"Okay," said Mr. Ruiz, "But what we need to…"

"Stop right there, Mr. Ruiz." Mrs. Thoreau held out her hand. "Don't say another word. You're dismissed, sir."

"What?" he asked.

"Just forget about everything," she said. "I'll take this case from here."

"I'll follow through with every court date," said Gabi.

Mr. Ruiz stood slowly. "This is trouble," he said.

—54

DALLAS WAS BROUGHT into the county jail. The arresting officer stood behind him as he was booked.

The guard looked over to Dallas. "Stand behind the line. Empty your pockets."

Dallas took deep breaths as he handed over his possessions: his wallet, keys, his phone.

"Tattoos?" asked the guard.

"What?" said Dallas.

"Tattoos?"

"Oh, none," said Dallas.

"No? I said, 'Tattoos'?" The guard's eyes narrowed.

The officer behind Dallas shrugged.

Dallas shook his head.

"Okay, I'll ask again. Do you have any tattoos?"

"No." said Dallas.

Another guard walked over.

Dallas' mind drifted, forgetting where he was.

"Are you aware of your rights, Sir?" said the officer.

"What?" asked Dallas.

"Have you been read your rights?" repeated the officer.

"Oh, yeah."

The guard beside Dallas grabbed him, "Here, come with me. You're entitled to a phone call. There're the phones."

Dallas shook his head.

"No. Over there – the phones…"

"I don't want a phone call," said Dallas.

"Nobody is going to know you're here," said the officer.

"Who cares?"

The officer scratched his head. "Okay." He directed Dallas into a small cell with six other inmates.

Two hours later, the inmates were taken from the holding cell, into an open area.

"Clothes off. Turn. Squat down and cough." The guard pointed to a guardhouse window. "Show your ass to her."

Each inmate stripped naked, turned, put their butts out, and coughed. Then it was Dallas' turn. He kept his eyes shut.

"Very good," said the guard. "Into the showers."

Dallas showered with four other men.

"Get clean. Use soap. Scrub that ass," yelled a large female officer.

Ten guards watched the men shower, as well as twenty more inmates.

Dallas' eyes darted back and forth.

Men were staring, laughing, giving signals.

Each inmate was handed a box with clothes, sandals, and soap.

"Can I have a bible?" asked Dallas.

"What?" said the guard.

"Can I have a bible?"

"Keep moving. Next."

The inmates all got dressed.

Dallas noticed his sandals weren't in his box.

He walked back to the guardhouse.

"Excuse me, my sandals aren't here," he said.

"Here," the guard passed a pair of sandals under the plexiglass window to Dallas.

"Keep moving."

—55

GABI OPENED her blanket, punched her pillow, and threw open the sheets.

She got in bed, pulled the covers over her, ran her hand through her hair, and closed her eyes, but she couldn't sleep. She stared at the clock, then the window, the trees blowing, the fence.

Gabi got out of bed, paced the room, went into the bathroom and turned on the light. She looked in the mirror, then turned the light off, and walked to the window, and opened it.

She stared out, noticed her red passiflora vines had spread out, taking over her garden.

I didn't know they grew so fast...

They don't stop.

Maybe I should cut them?

Gabi sighed, looked up to the moon standing over the ocean's waves, surrounded by endless darkness.

Her hand reached-up to the window. She watched it, one long movement. Then she decided to leave the window open.

Gabi drifted through the darkness, beyond the ocean, into the past, the years of her life, her marriage, the heartache, her children, her divorce, and then, way back to her childhood, that little girl with so many dreams. She put her hand across her chest to her shoulder.

What if...What if?

She sighed and stepped away, wondering if leaving the window open would be a mistake.

Then, she got in bed and closed her eyes.

—56

THE INMATES STOOD in-line for chow, a total of thirty prisoners, each with their own number.

Dallas was number fifteen. The man behind Dallas scratched his eye then stepped close to Dallas, who stepped forward and then turned sideways. The man again stepped closer.

Dallas rubbed his fingers together and wiped his chin. He took a step to his side, away from the man behind him. The man took a long step closer. Dallas looked directly into the man's eyes.

Two other inmates noticed Dallas was worried. He turned and faced the front of the line.

An inmate coughed.

Dallas rubbed his hands together. He knew what was about to happen.

Inmates nodded. One of them cracked his neck.

Dallas tapped his fingers on his thigh, planning his attack.

The man behind Dallas stepped on Dallas' toes.

Dallas didn't wait. He swung. Then, he elbowed the man in the head, pulled back, and punched him in the nose.

The inmates stood back, yelling. Dallas swung at another one, hitting him in his neck.

That was it. Everyone swung and kicked Dallas.

Dallas grabbed a guy around his neck, and then wrapped his arms around his torso, and charged forward with all his strength, lifting him up then slamming him down to the floor.

Six men grabbed Dallas and pulled him to the ground, pinning him down, kicking and swinging.

The alarm sounded.

By the time the guards got to Dallas, he was losing consciousness, only vaguely aware that the guards were dragging him away.

~   ~   ~

Dallas awoke in an isolation cell.

He sat up knowing he had at least one black eye and a swollen face.

Dallas ran his right hand over his left forearm. No blood. He set his hand on the floor.

His eyes searched the small, empty room and then went to the rectangular window in the door.

He stood, approached and then looked out the window. There was nothing to see except the white ceiling of the outer corridor.

He stood there, staring, placed his palm on the glass, and then down the door. Then he walked back and took a seat on the floor.

Dallas searched for something in the small room, anything, a crack in the wall, dust, something to look at, to think about. There was nothing but eight corners, no noise, no color, nothing, absolutely nothing, no faces, no voices, no darkness, no light.

Dallas leaned back against the wall, his eyes still searching.

His head drifted to the side. He let out his breath.

"Hello?" he said.

There was no sound, no echo.

"Hello? Anyone there?"

Still nothing.

His hands ran along the wall, solid concrete.

Oh God...

If I cry. Starve. Beg. Scream. There is no one, nothing.

"Can anyone hear me?" he yelled. "God, are you there? Can you hear me?"

Dallas' breathing got deeper.

He crossed his fingers and closed his eyes.

"I pray to you God. Are you there? Can you hear me?"

He opened his eyes, put his ear to the wall. Then, he sighed, leaving his ear against the cold concrete.

What's that?

He heard something. A sound. A vibration. He swallowed, closed his eyes and held his breath. It wasn't his imagination. There was a sound.

He held his breath again, moving his head down the wall to the floor.

It's down here...

What is that, someone talking?

Dallas crawled with his ear against the concrete floor. This way. No. That way. Searching. Trying to find it.

"It's a song. I knew it."

If he held his breath long enough, his ear could tune in, and he could hear the melody.

He crawled farther to the center of the cell, then backward, and then he held still. He took two short breaths, then one long one, and held it.

A minute later, his lungs were about to burst.

"Bob..." he said. "Bob...Bob...Bob..."

Dallas sat up took several deep breaths, then held it, then released. Then, he took one long deep breath, and put his ear back to the floor.

He held his ear there, completely silent.

Dallas began to sing Bob Marley's *Three Little Birds*.

He lifted his head from the floor, took another deep breath and put his head back. He hummed the melody. Tears of joy filled his eyes. He put his head back to the floor. Then, he sat up, laughing. He fell back on the floor, sprawled out, staring up, taking one deep breath after another.

Through his laughter, he screamed, "Fuck you all. Everything's gonna be all right."

—57

MR. RUIZ WALKED in the courtroom. He looked at Mrs. Hefernan, the bailiff who guarded the public entry, and smiled.

He took a seat next to her.

"Haven't see you in a while. Shouldn't you be by the plaintiff?" asked Mrs. Hefernan.

"They retired me from the courtroom. Mostly desk work now. Just, came to watch," he said.

Mrs. Hefernan looked puzzled. She leaned in. "Murder?"

Mr. Ruiz shook his head.

"Espionage?"

"No," he said.

"Murderous-love triangle? Oh yeah, you said 'No,' to murder…"

"Trespassing and harassment," said Mr. Ruiz.

"Trespassing? That's it?"

"Yup," he said.

The bailiff stared at Mr. Ruiz.

"I got a feeling 'bout this one," he said. "We'll see. It's the first on the docket."

Gabi was seated in the audience with her lawyer.

Dallas was brought in, his left eye still swollen and purple, wearing an orange jumpsuit, the number 8827 on the back. Cuffs and leggings restricted his movement.

A large bailiff stood beside Dallas. "Take a seat here."

"Yes, sir."

Dallas searched the audience.

"Sit down, Dallas," said the guard.

Dallas spotted Gabi. She turned away, and then coughed and straightened her blouse.

Mrs. Thoreau Esquire looked to Dallas.

"All rise," said the clerk. "The county of Hillsboro is now in session, the honorable Meredith Andrews judge presiding."

The judge entered.

"You may be seated," said the clerk.

"Okay, Jessica. Let's get started," said the judge.

"The people versus…"

The bailiff nearest the judge coughed and nobody, except those near the clerk heard Dallas' name.

"What did she say?" asked Gabi.

"Interesting name, sir," said the judge.

"Thank you, your honor," said Dallas.

"What was his name?" Gabi looked to her lawyer.

"Shhhhhh." Mrs. Thoreau Esquire shrugged.

"Please, all quiet in the courtroom," said the clerk.

Dallas tried to lift his hands to scratch his nose, but the chain from the leggings to his handcuffs prevented him.

The judge glanced at Dallas, while flipping through a stack of files.

"Prosecution, please come forward," said the clerk.

Gabi and her lawyer walked through the audience and took a seat at the table, next to Dallas. Gabi kept her head turned away from him, refusing to look his direction.

"Charges?" asked the judge.

"Civil and criminal your honor, trespass, mental destress, harassment…"

The judge continued to stare back and forth at Dallas and the papers in her hands.

"Okay. What's the plea?" said the judge.

Dallas' lawyer asked him to stand. They both stood.

"We plead not guilty, your honor."

The judge tapped her fingers.

"Hold on, your honor," Dallas said. "I didn't plead not guilty."

"What's that?" asked the judge.

"I didn't plead not guilty," he said.

"Legal counsel, please confer with your client," said the judge.

"Wait, your honor," said Dallas, "Can I ask Gabi a question." He turned to her. "Gabi, is this what you want? Is this what you really want?"

"I beg your pardon, sir," demanded the judge.

Gabi stared straight forward, still refusing to look in Dallas' direction.

Mrs. Thoreau Esquire stared at Dallas, shaking her head. "He's an idiot," she said to Gabi under her breath.

"I just want to talk with her. Look at me, Gabi."

The judge glanced back and forth from Dallas to Gabi and then back to Dallas.

"Shut up, Dallas," said Gabi.

"You're going to make things worse," said a voice behind Dallas. The leggings prevented him from turning his head, but he knew.

"Is that you Joy?"

"Dallas, you idiot. You're going to make things worse. Shut-up."

"What the hell are you doing here? We're divorced."

"I'm here to help you, Dallas."

"Oh, please stop helping me," he said.

Mrs. Hefernan, the bailiff, looked at Mr. Ruiz, who smiled and nodded.

"Should I be worried?" asked Mrs. Hefernan.

"No. They're all harmless," said Mr. Ruiz.

"This is… interesting," said the bailiff.

"Told you," said Mr. Ruiz.

"Gabi. Look at me," said Dallas.

"Order in the court. Order. All quiet." The judge's voice boomed. "All this stops right now."

"Sorry, your honor," said Dallas.

"Okay, Mr…" the judge looked at Dallas' paperwork. "Does everyone call you Dallas?"

"Yes, your honor," he said.

"Okay, Dallas. You will not address the plaintiff. Don't do it again. Do you hear me?"

"Yes, your honor."

"Okay. Sir, you're dealing with serious charges."

"Yes. I know. I just want to ask a question, and this case can be closed…"

"Closed?" said the judge.

"I just want to ask a question, your honor."

"Shut up," whispered Dallas' attorney.

"If your question is for the plaintiff, you must direct it to me." The judge pointed to herself.

"Okay."

"I advise you to shut up Dallas," said his lawyer.

"Can you ask Gabi…"

"Don't call me that," shouted Gabi.

"What am I supposed to call you, Gabi?"

"Mrs. Rogers."

"Stop. Stop," said the judge. "All quiet. I will not lose control of this courtroom."

"Your honor, I just want to ask her if this is what she really wants? You want me to be raped and killed in prison, Gabi?"

A burst of laugher began in the audience. Even the judge coughed and smiled.

"I'm not a gang member. And I'm pretty good looking, even though I'm forty, and I won't let anyone touch me, so they'll have to kill me. Is that what you want?"

The judge slammed the gavel. "Shut up, sir."

"Dallas, you're so stupid," shouted Joy.

Gabi shook her head.

"Shut up, Dallas," said his lawyer.

"One question is all I want."

"Please be quiet, Dallas," his lawyer insisted.

Dallas stared at Gabi.

"Please tell Dallas not to look at me," she asked her lawyer.

"I can't control where he looks," said Mrs. Thoreau.

The judge just shook her head. "Sir, you're about to get contempt added to your charges."

"Yes, your honor. I just wanted to ask Gabi…"

"Shut up, sir. This is your last warning."

Dallas stared, shaking his head, "Sorry, your honor…"

The judge gestured with her index finger and thumb – showing one inch. "You're this close to doing serious time."

Dallas tried to raise his hand, with his chains clanking against the table.

"Plaintiff, state your case."

"Your honor," said Dallas' lawyer, "We still haven't entered a plea."

"Ah, yes," said the judge.

Dallas raised his legs under the table, so his hands could be lifted.

The judge's gaze went back to Dallas. "This isn't a classroom, Dallas. What do you want?"

"I'd like to ask Gabi a question…"

"You'll not communicate with the plaintiff."

"Don't do this, sir," said a black woman in the audience.

Everyone looked at her.

"I'm trying to help the fool," she said. "Everyone else is giving him advice."

Mr. Ruiz couldn't help but laugh.

"Your honor," Dallas began.

"You're crazy," Joy interrupted him.

"Just ask her if she wants me to go to jail or marry me."

"Marry you? What?" said the judge. "Counsel, is your client mentally competent?"

Mr. Ruiz's eyes rose up to the bailiff. She frowned.

"Move over. I'm going to sit down with you," said Mrs. Hefernan.

Mr. Ruiz and Mrs. Hefernan both laughed as she took a seat.

"Whatcha think?" asked Mr. Ruiz.

The large bailiff put her hands up in the air. "I don't know," she said.

"You want me to defend myself, Gabi? Remember the promise…You made me promise. Remember?"

"You were the biggest mistake of my life," shouted Gabi.

"Is this what you want? You want me to go to jail? Just answer the question, Gabi."

"Evidently, that's exactly what she wants, sir. You got contempt."

"Yes. I do!" Gabi screamed.

Finally, there was silence.

Everyone looked around as if wondering what would happen next.

Dallas broke the silence. "I'm sorry I hurt you, Gabi. I was wrong. I should've never pushed you away. I'm trying to save you."

"I don't need to be saved, asshole." yelled Gabi.

"Look at me, Gabi. I'm sorry I didn't make it to São Paulo. I thought this would prove everything."

Mrs. Thoreau just stared at Dallas. She said, "Shut up," not bothering to hide the sympathy in her tone.

"Better save yourself," said Gabi.

"I love you, Gabi. Always will."

The judge stared back and forth at the two talking, with her hand raised to the bailiff nearest Dallas.

"I love you," said Dallas. His eyes went to the judge. "Your honor, I plead guilty to all charges."

"I give up," said the judge. "Counsel?"

Mr. Ruiz and Mrs. Hefernan just stared.

"You what?" said Dallas' lawyer.

"I plead guilty," said Dallas.

The judge stared.

"Shouldn't you do something?" said Mr. Ruiz to Mrs. Hefernan.

"I'm responsible for the back door. That's it," she said.

"I'm guilty of everything. Throw me in jail. I don't want this shit anymore."

Gabi's face turned red. She finally looked at Dallas.

The judge couldn't turn away either.

"You know what you're doing, sir?" asked the judge.

"Yes. This is what you want, right Gabi?"

"Dallas," Joy shouted. "You idiot."

The judge nodded to the bailiffs.

The bailiffs took hold of Dallas' neck.

He pushed back.

"Don't fight them," said Dallas' lawyer.

"I can't believe it," said Mrs. Hefernan.

Mr. Ruiz nodded.

The judge stared at Gabi. "I hate to do this…Oh well. Counsel?"

"You heard him, judge," said Dallas' lawyer. "We plead guilty."

"You're charged with contempt, sir. And your plea is accepted," said the judge.

Gabi couldn't turn from Dallas. Her hand covered her mouth. "How long will he be in jail?"

Mrs. Thoreau shrugged.

"Take him to jail," yelled the judge.

Dallas fought the bailiffs. A second bailiff crossed the courtroom and grabbed Dallas' arms.

"Don't do this," Joy called out to him. "Don't fight."

Dallas continued to struggle. Someone slammed his head on the table. He stared directly into Gabi's eyes.

"Sorry," he yelled.

"Dallas…" Gabi mumbled.

"I wanted to tell you…" he said.

The officer fought Dallas, slamming his head on the table again.

"I'm sorry…I tried…" said Dallas.

"The defendant will be silent." The judge was fighting a losing battle. "Get him out of here."

"I tried Gabi. I'm sorry."

Gabi couldn't turn away.

"I'm sorry, Gabi."

Tears formed in her eyes.

Dallas finally gave up his struggle. "I tried."

Gabi screamed, throwing up her hands, and Dallas was forced out of the courtroom.

"No," Gabi sobbed. "I want to drop the charges."

The judge smiled at her from the corner of her eye and shook her head.

Gabi cried.

"Your charges don't matter," said the judge, "He's going to jail for contempt."

Gabi covered her face and then fell back in her chair.

"What have I done? I'm sorry, Dallas."

"She loves him,." said Mrs. Hefernan to Mr. Ruiz.

He nodded. "I knew it," he said.

The judge pointed to Gabi. "Okay. Ma'am, you want to drop your charges?"

"Yes. Yes."

The judge tapped her fingers and shook her head.

"I can't believe this…" Mrs. Hefernan began to cry. "This is beautiful. It's true love."

The judge saw her bailiff, seated, crying on Mr. Ruiz's shoulder, in the back of the courtroom. She couldn't help but smile.

"He's going to spend some time for contempt," she said and sighed.

Mr. Ruiz handed Mrs. Hefernan a handkerchief. She blew her nose.

"You have made a mess of my court room, Mrs. Gabriela Rogers. You know that?"

Gabi covered her face again, "Oh my God."

"Mrs. Rogers. He might leave without serious time, but I'll be given a citation. Now, listen very carefully, if you call us – anyone of my police officers about this situation, who's going to jail, is you!"

"What will I be charged with?" asked Gabi.

"Obstruction of justice, young lady!"

Gabi couldn't believe what was going on – she felt tiny, like a small mouse caught in the grinding gears of an enormous machine; a pitiless monstrous engine that devours the weak.

"I can't…"

"No!" said the judge, "Not another word young lady. You leave here. I never want to see you in my courtroom ever again. Now go!"

—58

"GABRIELA, WE NEED to talk," said Mr. Medina, the general manager.

"We do?" said Gabriela.

"Yes," he said.

"Well... okay."

"Gabriela, this is a company lawyer, Mr. Lawrence."

"Nice to meet you," said Mr. Lawrence.

The two shook hands.

"Here. Let's go into the conference room," said Mr. Medina.

He opened the door, and the three of them entered.

"Now. I'm going to step outside. The conversation will be recorded, okay Mrs. Rogers?"

"It will?" Gabi looked around, wondering.

Both Gabi and the lawyer took a seat at a table.

"So?" she asked.

The lawyer ran his thumb and index finger over his bottom lip. "I'm going to be blunt. Do you understand that, Mrs. Gabriela Rogers?"

"Yes."

"What happened at the trial?"

"What do you mean?" said Gabi.

"I mean what's going on? You dropped the charges."

"Yes."

"So, what happened?" said Mr. Lawrence.

"Nothing," said Gabi.

"You called the police on this man. Now, I heard you dropped the charges?"

"So?"

"Does this man…How can I say this? Does he have something on you?"

"What do you mean?"

"Is he blackmailing you, Mrs. Rogers?"

"No. No. Of course not."

The lawyer's fingers tapped the table. "Is this the same man who sent you a package at our office?"

"Um…Yes," said Gabi.

"He pleaded guilty to your charges?" asked Mr. Lawrence.

"Yes," said Gabi.

"Why didn't he go to jail?"

Gabi sighed.

"Throw him in jail. He won't bother you again – or come around our office, right?"

Gabi coughed.

"Now, I know why my boss stepped outside," she said.

"Okay, let me ask you something else…"

"Yes?"

"I'm going to be blunt again."

"Please don't change on my behalf," she said.

"Are you in love with this man?"

"No. I'm not in love with him."

Mr. Lawrence put an elbow on the table and rested his chin on his fist.

"I've heard of crazier things," he said as he searched Gabi's eyes trying to find something.

"Mrs. Gabriela Rogers..."

"Yes?" she said.

"Can I give you a word of advice?"

"Personal or professional?"

"Both."

"No," said Gabi.

"Well, Mrs. Rogers, you need it," he said.

"How about the professional kind..."

"Either way, it's the same," he said.

"Okay."

"You throw this man in jail, or you marry him."

"Oh, please."

"Mrs. Rogers," he said. "I'm serious."

—59

JOY PICKED UP DALLAS at the airport and then drove him back home.

Dallas' mind was gone; staring off into the distance.

"Do you want to talk about it?" asked Joy.

"No," said Dallas.

"If you don't want to talk about, I understand."

"Do *you* want to talk about it?" he asked.

"No. I just thought you might. Thought it might help."

There was a long silence, and the sound of tires running over reflectors as Joy switched lanes.

"Well, you looked in her eyes. What did you see?" Joy glanced from the road to Dallas.

"She looked at me for just a split second. She was scared as I walked toward her. But I saw it in her eyes, clear as day…"

"What?"

"She still loves me."

"Ha. Yeah right. She called the police, and she still loves you. What a joke. You're an idiot."

"You asked me what I saw." He felt the anger surge in him. "From what I could tell, that's what I saw. She still loves me. She couldn't throw me in jail."

"Yeah. That was weird. You were lucky, could've spent months or even years behind bars."

There was silence again.

Dallas tapped the door's armrest.

"If I knew she'd call the cops, I would've asked her if what she told you was a lie," he said.

"What did she tell me?"

"She said we were soulmates."

Joy glanced at him with sympathy.

"There will always be regret," she said. "You were very lucky."

"No. That's not it."

"What then?" asked Joy.

"I don't think she lied," said Dallas as he took deep breaths. "I don't think she would lie about something like that."

"She just said that to have an excuse," Joy told him. "It was luck."

"Stop saying that. It wasn't luck."

"Then why did she call the cops?"

"Because she wants nothing to do with me," he said.

"You know why she wants nothing to do with you?"

Dallas turned to face her. "Why?"

"Because you stood her up. She wanted her revenge. And she's right, you know. I would too. Any woman would."

"I can't believe you just said that to me." Dallas shook his head and winced in pain. "Why did I stand her up, Joy? Why?"

"Don't start with me, Dallas."

He closed his eyes and took deeper breaths.

"You know, you and I are so different," she said. "Yeah, we never loved each other, did we?"

Dallas' mind was an impossible maze, every direction, everywhere he looked, every thought, up, down, far off into the distance, walls, walls, walls, solid, brick, stone, impenetrable, the labyrinth went on to eternity…There was nothing to say, nothing to do.

"I wish I was in jail." Dallas nodded in confirmation. "Yes, I wish she had put me in jail."

"How would I pay the bills. You have children."

"I wish a fucking gang member was shoving a shiv in my chest right now. That I can take. I should've stayed and demanded to talk with Gabi. I think I deserve it. I should've gone to jail, even if I died."

"Oh – my – God!" Joy said. "You are so fucking crazy. I'll never understand you."

"That's the fucking point, now, ain't it? It took you sixteen years to realize it. You don't' care who you go out with. A man is a man to you."

"Oh, and she was special?"

"Yes."

"She's perfect because you were with her for just a few hours. You're so naïve, Dallas."

"Yeah…" He stared out the window, at the scenery. "I believed your lies, right? I have to be naïve."

"I thought I was doing the right thing for the family," said Joy.

"Letting another man fuck you, and then lying to me about it for sixteen years. That was the right thing for the family?"

"What about ripping my towel off in the street? Naked for everyone to see. All our neighbors, Dallas."

"That wouldn't have happened if you told me the truth sixteen years ago."

"I was protecting you."

"Oh God. Please stop protecting me. Just tell me the truth."

"You're crazy. You're fucking crazy."

"No, Joy. You're completely insane."

"Me. I'm crazy." Joy scoffed. "You're the one who went to jail. Not me."

Dallas' hand formed a fist. His face turned hot. His whole body quivered.

"Look at you. You're going crazy right now." Joy began to laugh. "They should have put you in a mental institution. That's where you should've gone. Crazy."

They pulled up to the house. Joy turned off the ignition and glanced at Dallas. "Remember what you said to me before we had sex the first time? You said, 'I want you to know, I never want to have children and I never want to get married.'"

"Yeah, that's what I said."

"So, why did you marry me?"

"Because you got pregnant and told me you wanted me to marry you, remember? I wanted my son to have a father," he said.

Joy took the keys from the ignition.

"You never loved me. Admit it."

Dallas bit his lip. "Why did you sleep with that guy, Joy?"

Joy stared, shaking her head.

"This is all bullshit." Dallas got out of the truck and carried his bags inside.

The house was still in shambles; the hole in the drywall, pictures lying on the floor, plywood boards covering windows.

Dallas took a seat on the sofa and turned on the TV.

Joy went to the bathroom and put more make up on.

"You know, Dallas," she said, looking down the hallway.

"Oh no...What?" Dallas turned in her direction.

Joy walked out of the bathroom and then down the hall, and stood in front of Dallas.

203

"You're right about everything. How's that? And now, I'm going on a date. Bye."

She smiled and left the house.

Dallas sat there on the sofa. His eyes slowly closed.

The noise from the TV echoed.

He got up and walked out of the house to the backyard, grabbed his cowboy hat, and pulled it down over his eyes. Then, he sat on the deck with his elbows on his knees, his hands bracing his head.

The ground, the rocks, the weeds, shuffled beneath his feet. A cloud of dust floated into the air. Dallas' head sunk lower.

He reached out with his right hand. "Want to go for a walk?" he said, as he closed his empty grasp. He reached out again, thinking of the two of them at that motel. "Want to go for a walk?" His hand was still empty. Dallas looked up. "Do you remember this, Gabi? Want to go for a walk?"

Then, everything fell apart. Tears streamed down his face. His hand reached out, opening and closing as if holding something, anything.

Dallas found it hard to breathe. His abdomen, his lungs, his body buckled inward.

"Oh God, please help me. Please help me, God."

Donovan, his youngest son, walked outside and stared at him. "I didn't know cowboys cried," he said.

Dallas lifted up his cowboy hat and looked at his son.

"Come here. Let me hold you," he said.

He pulled him into his arms, and held him tightly, running his hands through the boy's hair.

"I'm sorry," Dallas said.

"Why?" asked Donovan.

"For everything."

"Are you going to stop crying, Daddy?"

"I'm gonna try," he said.

"Cowboys don't cry."

Dallas kissed the boy.

"This cowboy is crying, son," he said.

—60

LATE ONE FRIDAY, just before Dallas' shift ended, he got a service call.

A pickup was stuck on a beach up in Lago Vista. It was far away, but everyone was busy.

Dallas didn't hesitate.

"Yeah, I'll do it," he said. "I'm on my way."

To make the time pass faster, Dallas called his Romanian cousin, Maria, and they talked as he drove up Hwy 183 and then West on Hwy 1431.

Dallas explained everything, including the fact that Gabi called the police, and he almost went to prison.

"Needless to say," he said, "You were wrong. We didn't make love Maria." He laughed.

"You need to forget about her, Dallas. Move on with your life. Get over it, please."

Dallas shook his head, laughing.

She went on about the future. She envisioned Dallas would travel, but she didn't know where or why. As she spoke, Dallas drove past Cedar Park and Jonestown, out to the hill country.

He said goodbye to Maria when he found the pickup. It was buried to its axel.

Dallas dug under the truck for about thirty minutes, trying to find a place to wrap his chain. Then, he took another twenty minutes to winch it out.

When it rolled onto solid ground, the truck didn't start.

So, the owner asked Dallas to tow it to a shade-tree mechanic he knew in Jonestown.

Dallas was connecting the pickup to his tow strap, when he looked out between a set of hills, through a cove. The sun was low on the horizon. Light trickled across the lake. Dallas knelt to get a better look.

The owner of the truck walked behind Dallas.

"You think it's gonna rain?" he asked.

"Don't know." Dallas ran his hands over the dirt, grabbed a handful, and let it drain out.

"Sir, can you raise my car?" the man said. "I'm in a hurry."

"Oh, yeah. Sorry," Dallas said.

After the tow, Dallas stopped by Georgetown to drop some money off for his ex and see his sons.

He knocked on the door of the house, even though half of it was his. Joy answered.

"Oh, you," she said.

"Hello…" Dallas tried to hand Joy an envelope, but she turned away before seeing it.

She left the door open, so he walked inside.

"Here's the money, for this month," he said.

Joy turned. "You can set it down in the kitchen."

"Where are Aaron and Donovan?" he asked.

"Getting something to eat at Sonic."

"Aw, I wish I knew. I'd have made something on the grill for them."

"You don't have to do that anymore," said Joy.

"Yeah. But I want to."

"Dallas." She paused. "Let me ask you a question."

"Oh no." He didn't need any more drama from her.

"You never really loved me, did you?"

Dallas sighed.

"Did you always love Gabi?"

"I don't know," he said, eyeing the front door. He needed to get out of there.

"Were you always lying to me, when you said that you loved me?"

"Let's not go there," he said.

"I want to know the truth."

"The truth? You?" Dallas stood, shaking his head. "Don't do this. It's a damn rerun."

"You don't want to talk because I'm right," she said.

"No, you're really just feeling guilty," he told her. "You're going out. Having fun. You don't care who you date, who you fuck. You never did. You – don't – fucking – care! And you climbed out on that ledge and stopped me from seeing the woman of my dreams, the woman I loved. And *you* feel guilty. Well, you should."

Joy picked up a knife and held it to Dallas' chest.

"You're a fucking piece of shit liar."

"You stick that fucking knife at me?"

"You twist everything I say, you piece of shit," she shouted.

"What fucking part of 'I want a divorce – we should've never gotten married,' am I twisting?" he said. "Then you climb out on that ledge and tell me I'm a terrible husband and father."

"I don't have anyone," she sobbed.

"That was your choice. You chose to lie to everyone. I didn't hold a knife to you and tell you to lie."

"Everyone is leaving my life."

"I'm still here," he said. "And I'm still listening to your bullshit, aren't I?"

"I'm sorry, Dallas." She sighed and put down the knife.

"All right. I'm sorry too. This whole marriage was one great big tragedy."

Dallas looked to the door. Aaron and Donovan stood there, holding their food.

"Hi, guys," he said.

—61

DALLAS WAS WEARING a pair of plaid shorts, a cowboy hat, a tank top, and boots, and he was working on his unfinished deck, when Aaron approached.

"You know, you don't live here anymore," Aaron said.

"Yeah. But I own half this place." He smiled at his oldest son.

"We don't talk anymore," Aaron said. "I'm about to leave."

"Going into the military." Dallas smiled. "You're better than I am, son. Follow your heart. Instincts, never ignore them. Don't think too much." Dallas pointed to his head, "Concentrate. Work hard. But don't think too much. Assholes think. Real men use instinct. That means you have to fight. But fighting gets different when you get older."

Aaron stared at him. "Why did you make me watch Grandpa die?" he asked out of nowhere. "You didn't let me turn away. You held my head."

"What did you see?" Dallas asked.

"I don't know…"

"Never turn away, son. Never turn away. Grandpa gave you something."

"What?"

"A piece of his soul," said Dallas.

"I still have nightmares about it, Dad."

"Nightmares aren't bad. You have to have them. Maybe he's telling you something." Dallas stared into the distance. "He'll always be with you, Aaron. That pain will hold your hand in tough times. You have to have a strong soul."

Aaron's eyes narrowed. "I think I see."

"Life will tear you apart. Don't let them take what's inside."

"Dad..."

"Yeah?" Dallas asked.

"Do you love Mom?"

"Of course. If I didn't, how could I love you? She's half of you, son," he said.

"Sometimes, I hear you and Mom talking."

"Yeah?"

"What did you mean by tragedy?" he asked.

Dallas took a deep breath. "Tragedy is when your great uncle, who fought with Patton and died at the end of WWII in the Battle of the Bulge when he was just a kid...it's Grandpa in an Asian prison. Guys like you fight and live tragedies so guys like me can live meaningless lives."

"Your life wasn't meaningless, Dad," said Aaron.

Dallas laughed. "Thanks, son."

"It's true."

"Spoken like a man." Dallas grinned at his son, "Well, young man, what advice do you have for me?"

"I don't know," said Aaron.

Dallas smiled again. "Good answer. When the time comes..."

"Yes?"

"Be strong," said Dallas, "You have to be strong to be right. That's what nobody tells you. If you're right and weak, you'll be destroyed. Don't ever forget it. Come here."

Aaron approached him.

Dallas ran his hand through his hair the way he used to do when he was young.

"Just be careful out there. Stay alive."

He reached out and they hugged, awkwardly at first, and then, with all their strength.

—62

AS IT HAPPENS, when the conscience is guilty, the soul is a book, and our faces narrate emotion.

Dallas was in bible study when the topic of marriage came up.

Dallas burst up from the sofa, cutting off the conversation. "Listen. You talk about hell – family – this – that. That's how you see things. Family. Family. Marriage. Marriage. God and church, and you're telling me how to live my life the right way. Okay. That's fine. Listen. I'll roast in hell for eternity—with flames swallowing my body and my soul, with Lucifer playing ping-pong with my eyeballs before I get back with my ex. I swear to God. And, here's the thing. I'm doing it for my family. Yeah. That's right. I'm doing it for them. I have two sons. And if I see them in a loveless marriage, I'll kick their asses. Okay? She's the mother of my two children. She's my friend. I love her like that...But I'll never remarry her – ever. And maybe I should go-out and date. Listen. I'm forty-two years old. I'm not going on dates, wasting my time with someone I know won't work out. Lightning ain't gonna strike twice. I know. I found her. She saw things, understood things. Came from the same background. Ain't happening again. I'll try. But I refuse to waste my time, and make a mistake. The last one almost cost me my life. Won't happen again. If I see it's not going right – or I'll go to jail, or have to feed an entire family for twenty years – or you'll cheat on me...If you don't unlock the car door – it's lights-out. I swear. I'll be by myself for the rest of my life. You see, me and this woman, I still love her. We made it past all that stuff. We did it naturally."

"Dallas, sit down," said the pastor.

Dallas took a deep breath – staring at everyone. "No. No. It's okay." He didn't feel like shutting up. It reminded him of when he was in court.

"Dallas. Shut up for once. I've said this before." The pastor stood and patted Dallas on the back. "Jesus wants to walk with you the way you walk, Dallas. It's okay. We accept you, and we try to understand you. That's why we're here. This wasn't specifically about you, even if you felt that way. Okay?"

"Okay," said Dallas.

"The important thing is that you're walking with Jesus and not against him, and we know you're a good soul and love Jesus."

"I do," said Dallas.

"Then have a seat here."

"No. Let me go tonight. Okay? I'll be back next week, if that's all right."

The bible study group all spoke out, showing support for him.

"Thank you," said Dallas. "Have a good evening. Sorry for the outburst. I guess I said enough. Goodnight."

Love
Fate

—63

DALLAS GOT OFF WORK, threw his equipment in the back of his truck, and wiped the sweat from his face.

He got older. Still refused to date. Kept going to church, and he read the bible before going to bed, but no matter what he did, the ache was still there.

To Dallas, things were unsettled.

He was waiting, thinking, praying, watching for a sign to go and see Gabi one last time, or, the answer to his prayers, to be with her.

The sign never came.

He turned on the radio and Nickelback's *Far Away* was playing.

Dallas pulled his truck off the road, picked up his phone and called Joy.

"I called to tell you, I can't pick-up Donovan tonight and watch him this weekend," he told her.

"Don't do this to me, Dallas. I have things to do."

"I know. You always do."

"Yeah. You're not the only one who has plans," said Joy.

"I want to see Donovan," he said. "There's just something I have to do, and that's it."

"Oh, God. You're going to go and see her again. Right?"

"No. Well. Maybe."

"Don't lie to me," she said. "God, you are stupid. I'm done helping you Dallas. This time, she's going to throw you in jail. Is that what you want?"

"I know she's the only one I want to be with."

"Do you love her?"

"Yes, and…"

"And what?" said Joy.

"And I don't even know her," said Dallas.

"So, why do this?" she said.

"Like I said, she's the only one. I don't know anything else."

"Okay. Go. I'll have a babysitter watch Donovan," she said. "And I'm not going to bail you out. If you go to jail, that's it."

"Okay," he told her. "Bye."

"Dallas, wait." Joy sighed. "Good luck."

"Thanks," he said.

She said, "You're going to need it, Dallas," just before she hung up.

—64

GABI SAT AT A table, having lunch with friends. The conversation was typical and meaningless. Her cellphone rang. She looked at the number but didn't recognize it, so she sent the call to her voicemail.

Her cellphone rang again. She looked at it, and let it ring.

"Message received," appeared on her phone. She sighed.

"What is it, Gabi?" asked Laura, one of Gabi's friends.

"Nothing."

Gabi had a feeling she knew who it was.

Dallas' voice came on, "I have to see you one last time, Gabi – just one last time." That's all that was said.

Her phone rang again. She pressed end and got up from the table, telling her friends she had to go.

The calls continued, and she continued to ignore them until she couldn't take it any longer.

"I knew you'd call me eventually," she said and hung up.

The phone rang, over and over.

Finally, she listened to the message.

"Gabi, I'm at a restaurant. The one near your work, on the first floor. I'm waiting for you. I just want to see you one last time."

The phone rang again.

She answered it.

"Not again Dallas. This can't go on forever. Get on with your life. Don't call me again. I don't want to see you."

"I have to ask you something," he said.

"What?"

"Not on the phone," he said.

"That's the only way I'm going to hear you."

"All right," he said. "Did you lie to my wife when you said we were soulmates?"

There was a long silence.

"I'll be in the ground-floor restaurant in a few minutes. Come down, or I'll go up," he said.

"I'm not at work, Dallas, but I'll be there soon, and if you come up, I'll have security throw you out."

"I'll make them shoot me."

"They will."

"Good," he said.

"Well, if they kill you, we'll get the answer, if we're really soulmates." Gabi laughed.

"Then, I'm going to end it today, and we'll know."

"What do you want, Dallas?" she asked.

"I just want to see you – fifteen minutes. I have to tell you something."

"Oh, this is crazy. Is that it?"

"I...I...I want to smell you. See you walk by me. I want to hear you say my name. I want to hear you sigh. I want to hear you laugh, one last time. I want to look in your eyes."

"Stop," she said.

"I want you to stare at me, and then turn away. I want to spend the rest of my life wondering what you were thinking. I want to see your legs. I want to hold your hand."

"I'm not going to hold your hand," she said.

"Gabi," Dallas' voice broke. "I have to see you."

"No," she said.

Then, complete silence.

"We'll see," she finally said, and hung up the phone.

—65

DALLAS SAT IN his old truck, then got out and walked into the restaurant.

"Hello," said a man from behind a counter.

"Afternoon," said Dallas.

"You can sit anywhere."

"Sir, I'm not sure how long I'll be, but if I'm getting in the way, I'll make sure to leave a good tip," said Dallas.

"You waiting for someone?" asked the man.

Dallas nodded.

"Well I'm Joe, I'm the manager. Don't worry about a thing. We're not busy."

Dallas was there for an hour, and was sipping his second beer, when he looked up and saw a woman standing at the front door of the restaurant.

She looked inside, then hurried off.

Gabi! Dallas rose from his seat and ran out the door. Once outside, he looked around, but she was gone.

He went back in, shrugged at the manager, and took his seat.

"Sir, the bar is about to close," said Joe. "We're in a business district. Not a lot happening late in the evening."

"I understand." Dallas sighed.

Then, he turned, and from the corner of his eye, he saw a silhouette of a woman at the door, standing next to the checkout, by the manager.

The manager stared back and forth at the two.

Gabi was shaking in fear.

"Are you okay ma'am?" asked the manager.

She glanced at him but gave no response. Then she looked to Dallas.

Dallas looked like a trained lion staring at an unknown object. All emotions were present; fear, hunger, cowardice, love, pride, even anger.

The manager's eyes darted back and forth. He then nodded and stepped backward, out of sight.

Gabi crossed the threshold into the restaurant.

She approached him, and Dallas thought about standing, but thought better of it.

Gabi motioned for him to stay seated.

Dallas blinked in acknowledgment.

Gabi walked to the table in front of Dallas, sat down, and crossed her legs.

"You want to hear me say your name?" asked Gabi.

Dallas nodded.

She took out her phone, and acted like she dialed a number.

"Hello…Yes…"

She looked at Dallas.

"Dallas. Dallas was very nice," she said and ended the call.

Dallas smiled.

With that, Gabi shook her head *no*. Hope was leaving him.

She sighed, staring at Dallas, then turned the other way.

"No," Dallas said aloud.

One of the businessmen stared at them, making the pair realize how strange they must look.

Gabi tried to laugh but couldn't. She stood.

Dallas stood too. He went to approach her.

Gabi stepped back. "Don't make me run away from you. I don't want to, but I will."

They stared at each other.

"Please sit Dallas," she said.

He did.

Gabi smiled, and he sighed.

She walked around Dallas – to the table just behind him – took a seat and let her hand fall to the side.

Dallas reached back. He took hold of it.

"This is it," she said.

Dallas finally broke down. He took deep breaths. Tears streamed down.

The woman who had been sitting with the businessmen walked by them, staring, on her way out the front door.

Dallas didn't care, he glanced back.

Gabi's face was solid, stone, emotionless.

Dallas stared down at the floor.

"Don't do something stupid, Dallas. This is the last time. Promise?" she said.

"No," he said. "There's so much to say. Do you remember Tatuapé?"

"Yes. Of course," said Gabi.

"You're crazy," he said. "I'm crazy too. I sat there on your sidewalk, with the horns honking. I know that part of you. I lived there too. We're the same."

Gabi didn't say anything.

Dallas waited then said, "If you take anything from me returning to your life, take this. The risk I took, placing everything in your hands just to see you. I can't make it clearer that I love you, and if anyone is to be rejected, I want to be that one."

Gabi took a deep breath. "I don't care!" she said.

"Yes, you do."

"I don't want to hurt you Dallas," she said.

"I hurt you, and I'm sorry," he told her. "I couldn't go on living like that. I know you still love me. I should have gone to jail. I know it. You know it. Hell, everyone knew it. The sheriff, everyone." Dallas smiled.

"You never should have come back Dallas. Life doesn't wait for anyone," said Gabi.

There was a long silence.

Dallas' voice was weaker. "I knew I was going to go to jail, and I still came," he said. "Because, like I told you, it didn't matter to me."

"Okay."

"You think us being together was a sin..." he said.

"Please stop Dallas. You never know when to stop."

Dallas covered his eyes with his left hand.

"Gabi, I'm sorry, I didn't make it to São Paulo. But your husband was wrong. I didn't lie. I loved you, and still do. I did everything I could, and I couldn't go to my grave without you knowing it."

"Okay, Dallas."

"Okay?"

"Please let go of my hand," she said.

Dallas squeezed as tight as he could, while taking one last deep breath.

"You're hurting me, Dallas."

He let go, and Gabi slowly got up. She walked backward, away from Dallas, then around the table.

Gabi began shaking her head, staring at this man just sitting there.

"You wanna know something Dallas?"

Dallas looked around – unsure. "What?"

"You're a Goddamn idiot! Sit like this...Say this...Turn this way...And I'm stupid enough to do it! You think me doing this crap, or posing this way, or saying these stupid things means something?"

Dallas smiled, "Means something to me."

Gabi's life came forward, brought out through years of adulthood, calculations, motherhood, hardship.

"It's stupid! Everything you do – and did was stupid! This entire great big nightmare! Oh my God! People are trying to live their lives, didn't you know that? I have – or should I say – had a life! Until you came back into it, like a bull in a China shop!"

Gabi wiped away tears.

"Do you have any idea – God almighty! I was interested in you! I was even willing to talk with you. Boom! Bang! Here comes Dallas, smashing everything up. Destroying everything I felt for him – my entire life!"

Dallas was silent – staring.

Gabi jumped up and down.

"You obliterated everything – crushed it beneath you!" She stared at him, shaking her head.

There was a long silence. Everyone in the bar watched the two, but it didn't matter to either of them.

"My life was destroyed too," said Dallas.

"Stop acting like an innocent child. It's infuriating!" she mimed Dallas, "My life...oh my life...I am sad..." then stared. "Did you know I had a gun in my car, and was planning on killing you if you came near me? Did you know that?"

"Yeah, I knew it. But you wouldn't have used it," Dallas smiled.

"Yes. I would have!"

"Then why did you protect me? Why couldn't you put me in jail?"

Gabi's eyes focused, her nostrils flared, breathing heavy. "I don't know why I dropped the charges."

"Yeah, you do. You know more about this, more about me than I do. You always did – and you're a liar," said Dallas – it just came out – then he smiled again, his stupid childish grin.

There was complete silence between the two.

"Who gave you the right to say that to my wife – if it wasn't true? Was that a lie? Soulmates?"

"I don't know what you're talking about!"

Dallas couldn't help but smile again, like a child staring at a mess he made in a kitchen, when his parents came home.

"Fuck you, Dallas!"

Dallas began to laugh.

"It was all a mistake!"

"Bullshit!" said Dallas.

Gabi lowered her head and covered her eyes.

"Who are you!" she said with her head lowered. "What is this?"

"Listen," said Dallas.

"What?" she muddled under her breath.

"It just is. You know it. Whatever it is…" he shrugged. "This thing between us, it's there, and I can't stop it. I have no control over it."

"You are a child! And this isn't me. I have control over my life!"

He began to speak.

"Shut up!" Gabi cut him off, "Just shut up! I don't want to hear anything else."

Dallas stopped.

"We are adults, with lives. After a point, we don't choose how we live. It doesn't matter what was said fifteen years ago."

"Sixteen years," said Dallas.

"Don't talk!" Dallas shrugged and she continued, "We don't have a choice. I live my life from the choices I've already made. And that's without you and your childishness, and that's just the way it is!"

Dallas was still silent – staring, waiting.

"That's bullshit. And I ain't gonna shut up!" he said it. "You love me, and I love you. We can make this work. We can meet once a month, talk on the phone, email. We're adults, we can agree to limits and work things out," said Dallas.

"I don't trust you. You're too dangerous. And…I'm not listening," she said. "I can't deal with you."

"It's not that you can't deal with me. You can't control your feels for me. You in your bullshit fantasy world!"

"My world is bullshit?" said Gabi, "How many times have you been to jail Dallas? Ever kill anyone?"

"You live in a dollhouse – a world full of fake people drinking wine – they know it tastes like shit! They drink it so they can claim to be more sophisticated…It's all bullshit! This world of lies, hints, insinuations, where everything is fake! I am real. I am here, in front of you and you can't deal with it."

Gabi shook her head, as if trying to rid herself of a spell being cast, "Listen! Listen," she raised her finger, "Listen to me Dallas…"

Dallas cut her off, "You were there. You lived it. You saw it. You felt it. You know it!"

Gabi took one long, deep breath, "Talking with you is a waste of time."

"It was real Gabi."

"This conversation is over. I will not speak to you again, do you hear me, Dallas?" she demanded. "And let me tell you something else…"

"What?"

Gabi's eyes widened, "I don't love you! Do you hear me?"

"Maybe, but I love you." Dallas grew a smile, "Every day, for the rest of my life…" he began.

"It's too late!"

"Never."

"That's life," she said.

"I can't imagine going the rest of my life and never seeing you again."

Her shoulders fell, "How did we spend our entire life away from each other?" she asked as she began to back away. "What happened? Oh, this life…"

"I don't know."

Gabi lifted her hands in the air like she did in the trial, just giving up…and she walked away, then she turned back to Dallas, "Let me ask you one last thing?"

"Go ahead."

"What's your real name?"

"Ah, it don't matter," he said, then smiled again.

"You're not going to tell me?"

Dallas shook his head, "No."

Gabi stared, nodded and left.

He reached out. "Don't go!"

Gabi walked out the door.

"All this crap, everything doesn't make a difference! It doesn't matter!"

Dallas stared at the empty space and then screamed. He picked up the table and slammed it down, breaking it into pieces.

The two businessmen, still there, stood-up.

"Sir," said one of the men.

The manager walked out from the shadows and raised his hands, letting the men know it was okay.

"Gabi. Gabi," Dallas shouted.

Gabi heard Dallas' screams but kept walking. She took deep breaths, then with her face hidden by distance, she cried.

Dallas ran outside, staring at Gabi walking away.

She sensed him behind her but kept going, refusing to turn around.

"Gabi!" Dallas screamed again.

Mascara ran down her cheeks, as black tears hit the concrete sidewalk.

"Gabi!"

Gabi kept walking, she turned the corner, and finally stood in front of the office building. She glanced back where Dallas' truck was parked, remembered the hope in his eyes and then the sorrow as he lowered his head, after she told him to leave her alone. There was a disappointment she never saw in Trevor. No other man would do what Dallas did.

Gabi sighed, remembering the first time she and Dallas talked. A memory flashed briefly in her mind; the way they made love, stared into each other's eyes.

She suppressed so much since her divorce to protect her children.

Is Dallas dangerous?

He's so honest and dumb.

Gabi sighed again, her hands trembling.

No. No. Stop. I'm strong.

Then, she remembered how Dallas smiled at her; the honest love he had.

*His wife really did climb out on that ledge saying she'd commit suicide...*There was no doubt in her mind.

I'm never going to see him again.

She reached for the door.

"I love him," she said.

Dallas was in front of the restaurant, still standing, staring at the corner, confused, as if trying to understand a foreign language, life, death, why the universe existed.

She walked into the office building.

*What we had was real – I really do love him...*she said as she kept walking. *Oh well...*

Dallas walked back into the restaurant, and realized he'd destroyed a table.

"I'm sorry, sir," he told the manager. He walked to the table and tried to put it back together. "It looks like this piece fits here..."

But the screws are sheared off.

Dallas walked back to the manager and pulled-out his wallet.

"I'll pay for everything," he said.

The manager waved his hand. "No. I was meaning to get a new one anyway."

"No sympathy, sir." Dallas held out two hundred dollars.

"You have a good evening," said Joe.

Dallas put the money on the counter.

"Please. It's been a long time since I saw that...felt that...It was worth a broken table."

Dallas closed his eyes and waited for the world to change, but it didn't.

"I'll pray for you," said the manager. "What's your name?"

"Dallas."

"I will pray for you, Dallas."

"Thank you."

Dallas saw a uniform on the wall in a glass case.

"Is that yours?" he asked.

"Yes. Ten years. Marines."

"Thank you for your service," Dallas said.

The manager smiled.

Dallas walked out of the restaurant, and when he reached his truck, he leaned against it. Then he took off his hat, wiped his brow, and just stood there, looking around. Oddly enough, there was sorrow, but relief also.

His soul was amputated, but it was done, over. So, be it. Now, it was time to get on with life.

Dallas got in his truck, turned on the radio and fussed with the knob.

"Now, the National Anthem…" said an announcer.

A child began to sing, *The Star-Spangled Banner*, in a clear, high voice.

Dallas smiled, put his truck in drive, and pulled-out. Then, he began to sing.

His mind drifted into the distance, eyes searching, trying to find something – anything.

He chuckled to himself, about life, about pain.

*There's no sense…*he thought.

The pain doesn't matter – it just is – it's part of life.

He laughed more, to himself, about himself…

Wonder what she would've done if I grabbed her, and just kissed her? I'm so stupid, I only think those thoughts afterward…

He laughed.

"Yeah, I know I'm an idiot, and the funniest things is – she still loves me!" he couldn't stop laughing.

He turned down a street – fixed his rearview mirror.

"This world is so absurd," he kept talking aloud. "We should've never let women vote!"

After he said it, he closed his eyes – he was laughing so hard – and he stopped paying attention to the road, then rear-ended the car in front of him.

Both cars pulled to the side of the road – he put his truck in park.

"Damn," he said as he got out of the truck – but he was still laughing, "Just one of those days."

The woman that he rear-ended was already outside her car, "Look what you did!"

"I know. I know. It's all my fault."

THE END

Did you really think it was gonna end like that?

Of course not...

I'm a Goddamn American!

—65

YOU SEE, Dallas lost everything. He had to live in an RV for a while. But then he bought a small house in the country, and lived by himself.

And time went on.

A few months became a few years. Dallas kept his eyes open, and spoke to women – trying to find another Gabriela.

Then, one day, while working on his yard with his youngest son, a black Lexus stopped in front of his house. Dallas smiled.

Now, wouldn't that be neat?

He imagined it was Gabi, but knew it wasn't.

"Dad, there's someone there," said his son.

"I know. Just a stranger. Don't worry about."

Dallas shrugged, turned, and went back to his work.

"Hand me that shovel," said Dallas.

The car didn't leave, and the engine kept running.

Dallas was interested in knowing who was in the driver's seat, but he also knew it wasn't his business.

To be honest, he'd been through so much, he didn't want to think about it. His mind was turned off. He'd turned it off years before. He was done with fantasies. Dreaming about Gabi.

All he wanted to do now, was work.

Anyone can stop a car in front of anyone's house.

Don't worry about it.

He began digging, to plant a tree.

~   ~   ~

But the car just sat there, idling, waiting. Then, the driver door opened.

Nobody stepped out – not yet.

Dallas felt eyes watching him. His sixth sense made him a little paranoid, but he wasn't worried.

He glanced under his arm, to see. He couldn't help but wonder.

Finally, a woman emerged – standing to her feet – crying.

"There's a woman," said the boy.

Dallas knew who it was, but he wasn't sure what to do.

Everything in the past as a distant dream. He wasn't even sure if what happened all those years ago was real. Did he really do all those crazy things? Didn't he and this woman make love in Illinois? Did he really go to jail when he went to see her? Did he even know who she was? Did it matter? Aren't man and woman made for each other? Don't they fit together, and everything else finds its place?

Dallas stood.

"Who is she?" asked Dallas' son.

"Gabi. The father turned to the boy and said, "Don't say a word son. I want you to watch this. Remember it."

Gabi and Dallas made eye contact, but they were far away, and neither of them moved.

The son followed his father's instructions – was quiet.

Within both Dallas and Gabi, was the urge to touch, a want of an emotion they denied themselves for years, because they couldn't find *the* person.

Dallas knew he had to wait. He didn't move a muscle, but their eyes didn't leave each other's.

Gabi took a step forward – her thoughts wondering.

Then she said something.

"Is this okay?"

Dallas smiled.

"I've been waiting," he said.

Gabi broke. The emotions were too strong. Body trembling. Words were gibberish.

"I…I…I don't…I can't believe I'm here," she finally said.

"I can," said Dallas.

She walked forward. He was covered in dirt, from work.

~   ~   ~

The two were older. They'd spent a lifetime apart. They were in their late forties.

Dallas slowly walked toward Gabi, and Gabi was reassured, then went to him.

They embraced.

She closed her eyes, then opened them, to see if it was real. If Dallas was holding her. He was.

"It's been so long," she said.

"I'm sorry."

"Life is so short!" she cried. "Why do this?"

Dallas took a deep breath – a breath of pain – of truth.

"Why didn't you come to São Paulo? Why did you stop talking to me? We spent our entire life apart. We didn't have kids. You wasted both our lives. We could have been together all this time. We would have been happy. We could have lived! Enjoyed each other. You wasted our lives!"

The anger was real – honest.

"I can't answer your questions Gabi," he shrugged.

"It's been so long."

"Yeah, I know," said Dallas.

Gabi lost eye contact, lowered her head, but she was still in his grasp.

"I ah…" now it was Dallas' turn to stumble. "I don't…I can't tell you anything that will fix or change the past Gabi. I can tell you, I'm sorry."

She sighed.

"God," she buried her head in his chest.

Dallas finally ran his fingers through her dark hair.

"I love you," she said.

"I love you too Gabi."

And that, ladies and gentlemen, is how it ended.

The End

KELLY MICHAEL VELAYAS

Velayas was taken to Venezuela at the age of seventeen. He arrived two years after Hugo Chaves' failed coup d'etats. The young Velayas watched for three years, from 1994 to 1997, as the country fell under communist control.

Velayas relocated to Brazil at twenty, traveling down the Amazon, then the coast to São Paulo. Living in Brazil off and on for twenty years…

Velayas' ancestors include a Warden of San Quentin prison, cowboys in Wyoming, performers in vaudeville, actors in Hollywood, soldiers in the Civil War, WWI, WWII, Korea, and Vietnam. His great-grandmother crossed the plains by covered wagon with five children, settling in Modesto, California, where Velayas was born.

He's worked as a clerk, teacher, filmmaker, lineman, ditch digger, and cable guy, in the US, Brazil, Venezuela, Paraguay, and a Caribbean island.

Velayas calls Texas home.

Made in the USA
Columbia, SC
16 February 2025

53884139R00143